MAGICA RIOT

KARA BUCHANAN

Copyright © 2024 by Kara Buchanan
All rights reserved. No part of this book may be reproduced in any manner whatsoever without written permission except in the case of brief quotations embodied in critical articles and reviews.
ISBN-13: 979-8-218-52008-3 (Hardcover), 979-8-218-52270-4 (Paperback), 979-8-218-52009-0 (Digital)
First Printing, 2024
Official page: magicariot.com
Artwork and logo design by Amber Dill - ambisweetiepie.com

Special Thanks

This novel would not exist in nearly the same form as it does now without the help of three very wonderful human beings.

My story editor Rowan Church was instrumental in helping me shape the many, many ideas I conjured up for the *Magica Riot* universe into a first novel that sets up this queer magical girl adventure. It was the difference between an idea and a story, and I am eternally grateful.

My copy editor Steph Buchanan polished the resulting words with a professional's eye for detail. In addition, she provided all of the lyrics you will read in this book. *Magica Riot*'s musical voice is, in no small part, her voice. I'm so very glad I was able to bring that voice to you.

Finally, my artist Amber Dill took my words and descriptions of our musical magical heroines and gave them life. She brought Claire, Sara, Cass, Hana, and Nova to reality so well that it altered the story itself, for the better. It means so much to me that you can see my girls with your own eyes, and they're exactly how I imagined them.

Magica Riot lives because of the help I had, and I give infinite thanks for that.

Kara Buchanan
September 2024

PART ONE

Claire

PART ONE

| 1 |

My Friday evening began in the usual fashion: trying to be invisible to the people around me as I waited for a girl to show up and make me seem cool enough by association.

I'd come downtown to the Clarion Room—one of the city's old music venues, made of creaking wood and dusty brick—to see a band called Magica Riot. My best friend, Hazel, had gotten me into them. I was a late arrival to their fanbase, but they'd quickly become my favorite Portland band.

Hazel was also the girl I was waiting for, and the girl who'd just called me to let me know she couldn't make it.

"I'm really sorry. I need to cover someone's shift at the video store tonight, and I could use the money, y'know?"

"That's totally okay, Haze," I said. "I understand. I'll tell you all about it tomorrow."

"Thanks! Curious to hear how they do."

"You say that like you're not sure."

"It's just that things have been rough since they lost Iris. I dunno. I hope they turn it around."

The band's keyboard player, Iris, had passed away two years ago. At least, that was the general feeling; officially, the police said she was "missing." I only ever got to see them as a four-piece, but I knew a lot of the original fans said they just weren't the same. I still thought they were incredible, but I had to admit, I felt a twinge of sadness that I'd never be able to see one of those old performances for myself.

"I'll let you know. It's not gonna be as much fun without you."

"Naw, man, you don't need me. Have a beer or two! Talk and mingle!"

I frowned, even though she couldn't see me. "I'm terrible at both of those things."

"No arguments! Go enjoy yourself. Do that sensitive shy nerd guy thing you do."

I smiled at her compliment even as I winced inside at being called a guy. The term had always felt like a straitjacket and a lie, not that I'd ever admit it.

"Yeah, of course. Don't work too hard."

"Never! You know me. Have a good night!"

"You too, Haze. Bye."

"Bye," she said, and the call ended.

There was no sense waiting around outside anymore, so I handed my ticket and ID to the girl checking them at the door. Once I was inside, I avoided the ancient, slow elevator, choosing the stairs instead.

A modest crowd had already gathered in the ballroom. Magica Riot didn't pull the same size audience they used to; besides the loss of their fifth member, they'd developed a habit of cutting shows short and bailing on gigs. Those kinds of things always made the casual fans start looking elsewhere.

So much the better for me tonight. Socializing was one of the things I liked least. I always felt out of place anywhere I went, and just inhabiting spaces seemed like a chore. My body was too tall, too wrong. I was 5'10" and tried to make every inch as unnoticeable as possible, from my nondescript jeans and T-shirts to my short, generic brown hair.

If only Hazel could have been here. She was so cool. I wished I could be like her, in many ways. I'd always thought that, but I'd never faced it, and I wasn't about to start now.

I resigned myself to being alone in the crowd, and made my way toward the bar to order a beer. I never drank much, but it'd help to pave over the anxiety.

* * *

I'd managed to get about halfway through my beer when a pale, energetic young woman bounded up, leaned on the bar, and waved to the bartender.

She was just a bit shorter than I was. Her outfit was as bright as the grin on her face: a pink tank top that accentuated her strong, wide shoulders, and a black miniskirt over pink fishnets. Her hair was dyed a matching pink and pulled up into fluffy twintails. An "X" in black marker on the back of her hand told me she wasn't old enough to drink alcohol, and even though I was just 22, that made me feel kind of ancient.

I knew instantly who she was, and it didn't help my growing anxiety. Her name was Nova, and she was the drummer of Magica Riot.

"Heya," she said as the bartender approached, "can I get a couple more Shastas for me and my bassist?"

The bartender, the kind of painfully cool girl with assorted piercings and a beanie who are the structural backbone of the Portland food service industry, smiled and nodded.

"Sure thing, I got ya. Give me just a sec."

Nova bopped her head to the house music and tapped out the beat on the bar top, which set her twintails gently swaying.

I didn't want to be awkward, but I also didn't want to miss the chance to tell her how much I loved Magica Riot's music. The sheer terror of being perceived was very real, but I had just enough alcohol in me to press onward.

"Uh, excuse me," I said, "you're Nova, right?"

She turned to me, a broad grin still affixed to her face.

"That's me!"

"I just wanted to tell you that I really love your band. Big, big fan."

"Right on! Thanks, man. I appreciate it!"

I probably should have stopped there, but I felt a little brave.

"Loved y'all ever since my friend played me 'Gender Hypocritical' one night. So good."

"Aw, thanks! I love that one, too. Sara's vocals are so intense, y'know?"

I kept going without realizing what topic I was dancing toward. "For sure, yeah, it really got me super emotional."

Nova gave me a curious look, so quick I almost didn't notice. I immediately regretted saying that, convinced I'd been too much by making a vague, sideways acknowledgment of my many personal gender issues, and tried to change the subject.

"Also, uh, I love what you all did with the chord progression in the bridge. Totally caught me off-guard."

"You know music and stuff?"

"I know some," I nodded. "I play keyboards. Not, like, in a band, or whatever. Not since high school."

She beamed at me. "That's awesome! You ever think about gettin' back into it?"

I shifted on my bar stool. "Well, I wouldn't say no, I guess. Don't know if I'm really cut out for being in a band."

"Hey, you never know! Might surprise yourself! Maybe you gotta change whatever's in the way, know what I'm saying?"

A weird pang of anxiety hit me. "Um, not rea—"

The bartender returned with the Shastas, interrupting my thought before I could finish. Nova thanked her before turning her attention back to me.

"I gotta run, but for real, thanks for the kindness, Keyboards," she said, as she slid off the bar stool. "I expect to see ya front and center right up by the stage, alright? I'll put 'Gender Hypocritical' on the set list for ya!"

I felt myself blush a little. "Awesome. Can't wait."

"I mean it. Front and center. I'm gonna make sure!"

"I promise."

"Good. I'm making ya our honorary lady tonight, since I can tell you've got the heart of a maiden."

She winked at me, and I felt a flutter in my chest. I had always dreamed about being a girl, but I never openly shared that with anybody. Was she onto me? Or was I just overthinking things? Either way, I couldn't shake the feeling that she could see right through me.

Before I could form a reply, she had breezed past, headed for the backstage access door.

I got up from my bar stool and made my way toward the stage. Whenever I went to these things with Hazel, she was outgoing enough for the both of us. Without her, though, I usually fell into some bad habits.

I'd try to stay in the back of the crowd, preferably off to the side and deep in the shadows. I'd stand with my shoulders hunched, my head down, and my hands in my pockets, doing my best to not be noticed. Basically, I was terrified of taking up space. It felt bad having a bunch of people looking at the version of me I was stuck with, because I doubted I'd ever muster up the courage to change it.

Tonight, though—maybe I could make an exception and stand up at the front of the stage. Nova *had* requested it, after all.

As I made my way through the crowd, the house lights dimmed, the background music slowly faded out, and the members of Magica Riot walked out into the rainbow-hued stage light.

The band's lead singer and rhythm guitarist stepped up to her microphone. Sara Ward's whole aesthetic always seemed impossibly cool to me: tall and strong-looking in tight jeans, the sleeves of her red button-down shirt rolled up, with a head of short auburn hair that glowed in the stage light. Around her neck, she wore a short lavender scarf tied as an ascot, which made her look more than a little princely.

People said she seemed much more restrained these days, since Iris was gone. Having never seen them in person at their peak, I could only go by old videos. She did seem quieter and less exuberant now. I'd never focused too much on it, since it was completely understandable, considering what the band had gone through.

Sara looked out across the room and gave a small nod. "Hey, friends. Thanks for coming. We're Magica Riot."

With that, Nova counted off a beat, and the band launched into "Like You," which wasn't something I was prepared for right at the start. That song was one of my favorites, and nearly always made me cry.

It was also the last single they'd released as a five-piece, and the last song written by Iris.

My gaze was drawn to Hana Hasegawa, the bassist. She and Nova made for a formidable rhythm section, effortlessly locking in together like two gears, in perfect sync. Yet, as individuals, they seemed like complete opposites. Nova's energy crackled like electricity, while Hana exuded a calm and cheerful demeanor, swaying to the beat of her bass and Nova's kick drum. Her long, dark brown ponytail bobbed and swayed with each nod of her head. But it was on her instrument that she truly shined.

As Sara stepped toward the mic and her voice filled the air, I felt my heart ache with longing. I had always been drawn to female musicians, envious of their ability to express themselves so freely through their art. In my daydreams, I imagined myself joining them on stage, finally able to show the world my true self.

I couldn't linger on that ache for too long, so I pushed those thoughts to the side and zeroed in on the lyrics as Sara sang.

I always do things the hard way, can't fall in line right now, oh maybe someday, try to smile and do what I'm told, don't step out of line or be a little too bold.

Identity, self-image, living as yourself. Anytime the band's songwriting turned to those subjects, I felt tears well up in my eyes. Why shouldn't girls—of all kinds, however they got to be girls—get to be exactly who they wanted to be? Why shouldn't they live free and happy without society cutting them down? I believed that, as strongly as I ever believed anything. I wanted to fight for them. I want to be—

At the chorus, Sara's voice blasted out across the room.

What's it like to be like you? What's it like to be beautiful and true?

My breath caught in my throat and I pushed back my tears; at the same time, I glanced down from Sara to the back of the stage. My eyes caught Nova's as she drummed.

Without breaking the beat, she grinned at me, that same odd grin she'd given me at the bar, and shot me another wink. For just a moment, I felt warm inside in a way I couldn't quite process.

My mind drifted for a moment, and before I knew it, the chorus had ended and Cass Coates, the lead guitarist, was launching into a short solo to segue into the next verse. Cass was an exceptional musician, with precise, laser-like skills on the guitar. She also looked effortlessly cool, like a true rock star. As she played, the rolled-up sleeves of her yellow flannel shirt accented her toned arms and dark skin, as her twist-out hairstyle cascaded over her eyes. Together with Hana's bass counter-melodies, their interlocking parts created a perfect harmony between guitar and bass riffs.

By the time she'd finished and Sara had gone into the second verse, whatever lingering anxiety I had about being at the front of the crowd was gone. I left myself drift along on the music, let the beat pound and thump against my chest as the guitars snaked around me. It almost felt, for the rest of the set, like I was one with the song.

I wished I could feel that feeling all the time.

The band powered through the rest of the set, playing favorite after favorite while I stood transfixed at the front of the crowd. With each passing song, I felt my emotions build into a high I knew I'd eventually crash down from, but I rode it for as long as I could.

During the final song, Sara's voice soared over thundering drums and wailing guitars, and suddenly broke into a tormented, aching scream that pierced through the crowd. I felt the energy in the room shift into unease and concern. People stopped nodding along to the beat, and a hush fell over the room.

A beat later, it was gone; Nova smashed her drum kit and Cass ripped into one last solo, bringing the mood back around. The smallish crowd clapped and cheered; I joined them, heart pounding, completely caught up in the moment.

With a crash of Nova's cymbals, the final song came to an end. Sara took the mic one last time and nodded to the room.

"Thank you, friends. We've been Magica Riot. Be good to each other."

It was a short set, barely twenty minutes, but it hit me like a truck all the same.

After the set, the band took down their gear to move it off stage as a small group of diehard fans gathered around for autographs. I desperately wanted to go over and tell them how much I loved the show. My mind raced with thoughts and scenarios, practicing them in my head, trying to come up with a way to approach them without seeming weird or desperate. A way to just seem like a normal, functional human being.

But my anxiety got the best of me. Those fans were all much cooler and more interesting than I could ever hope to be, and I couldn't bring myself to join. After several long, agonizing moments, I let out a sigh and headed to the bar to close out my tab and avoid any potential awkward interactions.

After I closed out, I headed for the door without looking back at the stage. Right before I reached the door, I nearly collided with two guys dressed in flannel and jeans who were standing together at the back of the room. I muttered an apology, but neither of them responded. They both glared at me in a way that was intimidating and strangely vacant. Since they were also both noticeably bulkier than I was, I decided it was best to just move along.

I pushed through the bar's front door and exited onto the sidewalk. The summer air in downtown Portland was warm and still, which meant I'd be sweating by the time I got to the MAX station. I frowned at the prospect; it'd be best to take it easy the rest of the way home.

Soon, I got the feeling that somebody was following me.

I'd cut down a side street between two office buildings looming in the dark above me, emptied out for the evening. A block over, bars and restaurants were open and attracting crowds, so I knew that here, I wouldn't have to walk through the Friday night rush. The downside was feeling alone and isolated from the safety of crowds, but I had never felt all that nervous walking around downtown at night.

Until now. I picked up my pace, and as I neared the end of the block, I glanced back over my shoulder, hoping to dispel my paranoia.

I spotted them immediately: two bulky figures, silhouetted against the distant streetlights. My encounter leaving the club was more consequential than I'd hoped.

I considered my options if the situation took a bad turn. The MAX station wasn't that far, so conceivably, I could just turn right at the end of the block and head back to the Friday crowds for the rest of my walk. Safety in numbers and all that. I didn't want a confrontation; my main goal was to be left alone to live my life, free of bruises and wounds. I never thought that was too much to ask.

I dared another glance, and couldn't help but notice the two figures were startlingly close now. Much closer than should have been possible. How the hell had they closed the distance so quickly?

I was just about to break out into a run when I felt a powerful hand clamp down on my shoulder. The city spun as my body slammed into the building's wall. A shock of pain radiated through me, and I found myself pinned. The impact rattled me, and it took a moment to refocus.

But once I did, my blood ran cold. The two guys from the bar towered over me, their blank expressions and empty eyes regarding me with clinical disconnect. That strange vacancy struck me again; it was as if they were only going through the motions of being human.

"Whoa, whoa, whoa," I said. "I don't want any trouble, okay?"

Silence. Not a muscle so much as twitched on either of their faces.

"Seriously, whatever it was that I did, I'm sorry! I promise I didn't mean to do it!"

Nothing.

"If you want my wallet, you can take it! There's hardly anything in there anyway! Just let me go!"

At this, finally, I got a reaction. Unfortunately, it was far worse than I could have possibly imagined.

The one on my right—the one not pinning me to the wall by my shoulder—raised his hand. With the most sickening wet crunching sound I've ever heard, his hand split apart and dissolved, revealing a shimmering chromatic silvery-white spike.

The sharp tip of the spike gleamed even in the ambient city light. A pattern of holes formed around it, as though the spike was meant to penetrate into something and extract things from it, or inject things into it.

I did not want either of these to happen to me.

I opened my mouth, but my voice failed. Fear paralyzed me. The man—the *creature*—raised its spike and aimed it at me. An energy radiated from it that chilled some ancient part of my mind.

It pulled back and prepared to strike, but it never got the chance.

| 2 |

"No flammin' way, jerks!"

The creatures were suddenly flung back through the air, landing on the pavement a good twenty feet away with a loud smack. My jaw dropped, and remained there as I noticed Nova standing where the creatures had just been, her twintails swaying in the breeze. She grinned and gave me a little wave.

"Ugh, I knew I had a scummy feeling about tonight. You okay, Keyboards?"

I stared back and blinked slowly. "I don't even know how to begin to answer that."

She laughed. "That's totally fair! I'm gonna deal with these losers, 'kay? You'll be fine. I just need you to get back and let me work. Grab a hiding spot for me."

She pointed toward a pair of grimy dumpsters against the wall, signaling me to go there for cover. My mind was still reeling from the sudden turn of events, unable to fully process what was happening.

"Nova," I stammered, my voice shaking. "What—what the hell is happening?"

Out in the street, the creatures struggled back to their feet. Their human forms fell apart as their skin ripped to pieces. Wet scraping sounds accompanied every movement. Whatever false viscera and tissue had been concealing their true appearance began to glop off of their bodies and onto the pavement, dissolving as more of their chromatic silvery shells emerged.

Nova grinned at me. "No need for language! Just get to cover! Things are gonna get serious-style unpleasant in a hurry. I gotta teach these jerks a lesson, in a dismemberment sense."

With loud snaps and squelches, the creatures' human heads shattered. Hair, eyes, bits of skull, it all disintegrated. New heads as sharp and pointed as their arms appeared in their place and sprouted four ink-black orbs. As their mouths transformed into dark circular openings, thick shells burst from their chests, breaking through flesh and bone with a sickening wet crack. Every step they took sent shivers down my spine as the sound of their transformation echoed against the surrounding buildings.

"What are those things?" I asked.

"You're better off not knowin' right now. Just get back! I gotta do a thing real quick."

"I don't understand!"

"No arguing! I ain't gonna let you get hurt on my watch!"

She grabbed me, and I felt a jolt. Ethereal light filled my eyes, radiating warmth that seemed to seep into every fiber of my being. Visceral, ancient sensations penetrated deep into me, down into my very cells.

"Okay, yeah, thought so," Nova said, more to herself than to me. She smiled. "It's okay, Keyboards. You just gotta trust me, alright?"

I was so enraptured by the sensations flowing into me that I didn't protest.

Nova sat me down behind the dumpsters and turned her attention back to the creatures. They were now unrecognizable as anything resembling human, their bulky chitinous shells having completely replaced their disguises. Blood and bits of liquified flesh slid off them as the hard, chromatic surface underneath gleamed in the streetlights.

Not that this concerned me now, as I was experiencing some kind of supernatural trip. The fear and confusion that had consumed me just moments before had dissipated, and a sense of security and benevolence settled in its place. It grew stronger with each passing moment, sending warm, joyful tendrils of tranquility through my mind. I had never felt anything even close to this. It was as if all my worries were being washed away and replaced with a blanket of pure serenity.

"Trust, yeah," I managed, though I didn't know if she heard me. "I trust you, Nova." It was almost a realization.

As the creatures approached her, Nova lifted her wrist to her mouth and spoke into a watch-like device I hadn't noticed before.

"Hey cuties! I've got a little after-party sitch with a couple of Pandoras near Thirteenth and Alder. Anybody wanna join the fun?" She turned and gave me an awkward thumbs-up. I wasn't sure if I should return it.

A moment later, she raised her hand skyward. In a new development in the evening's things-that-seemed-impossible festival, a glittering microphone covered in blue jewels appeared out of thin air, and she grasped it. She lowered it to her lips and shouted into it at the approaching creatures.

"Maidensong harmony power ... go live!"

Out of nowhere, a dazzling burst of electric blue energy engulfed her. The air crackled with raw power. I could barely perceive a rush of motion, but it was too swift for my eyes to track. Then, just as suddenly as it had appeared, the vibrant explosion dissipated, revealing a figure in its center. It was a girl in a sleek black jacket adorned with bits of blue. Her skirt, starting short and angling out to a longer length at the back, was a striking contrast of jet black with blue trim. Tall punk boots adorned her feet, reaching up to her knees, and studded fingerless gloves completed her look.

I could tell it was Nova, but her presence had completely changed. She fearlessly stood in front of the approaching creatures and raised her arm, pointing straight at them. When she spoke, she *spoke*.

"I am a guardian of song and heart! Servants of the darkness, be silenced by the song of Riot Blue!"

The creatures lunged at her. With shocking speed, she dodged the first and swung her fist at the second. Her punch landed square in its chest, which once again sent the creature flying back. The first creature, meanwhile, staggered as it missed her and spun around in an attempt to reorient itself and try again.

Nova held up her hands. In a burst of glittering blue light, two drumsticks materialized in her grasp. Several phantom discs, like holographic drum heads, materialized around her. She started to play, hammering and pounding at the discs with precise fury, and I recognized the beat of "Down in the Lilies," a song off the band's last album. Blue energy crackled and sparked around her in time to the rhythm.

She glared at the creature she'd dodged as it prepared another attack.

"You want some? You can't handle it, creepo!"

The holo-drums pulsed and glowed as she unleashed a monster drum fill and a crash of the virtual cymbals floating in front of her. A huge shockwave rippled out of the drums and smashed into the creature. It went flying into the wall of the building nearby. The sharp crack of chitin on concrete rattled my bones.

The other creature she'd punched had regained its footing out of her line of sight, and it looked like it wanted revenge. It rushed over in my direction and jabbed its spiked arms into the dumpster

I wasn't hiding behind. It lifted the entire thing above its head, and ran toward Nova, her back still turned.

I tensed as a realized what was about to happen and tried to call out to her—but before I could, the entire world slowed until the scene in front of me was at a standstill.

A loud ringing pierced my skull and reverberated down through me. I reached up to touch my head, but I had no command of my body. Dizziness swept over me, and I smacked against the rough metal of the dumpster for stability. I fought for control, but I felt impossibly small and helpless, and the ringing only intensified. It punched deeper, like a blast of ice water into my core.

From a place beyond the reaches of my consciousness, I heard a faint noise, distant yet unmistakable in its presence. It seemed to echo from another dimension, beckoning to me, and I strained to make it out.

Y... an... av... r...

"What did you say?" I couldn't tell if I was speaking out loud or only thinking.

The voice spoke again, close and clear, a whisper in my ear that hushed the din outside.

You can save her.

"Save her? I can't save her!"

You can save her. You carry the pure heart of a maiden.

"What are you talking about?"

Listen to the song, and awaken, young maiden.

I shook my head.

"You've got it wrong! I'm not a maiden! I'm just a guy."

I know what you are, even if you deny yourself.

The words pierced my heart, a precision blade slicing straight through me.

"I don't want her to get hurt, but I can't do anything."

Open your heart, and listen to my song.

"Your song?"

The Maidensong will give you the power to save her. Open your heart.

Tears filled my eyes as I struggled to make sense of the voice's words. Nova was in danger because of me, and it didn't sit right with my conscience. I would do anything to protect her, but at that moment, I felt utterly helpless.

That warm sensation spread through me once again, this time concentrated at my right hand. Slowly, I raised it up to examine it, feeling drawn to the source of the warmth. There, shimmering in my palm, was a microphone adorned with glistening purple jewels. As I grasped it, its purpose became clear—it was a conduit, a means for me to tap into something much greater than myself.

As if in reaction to my realization, a jolt of energy rocked my body. The most beautiful song I'd ever heard started to build inside my ears, pushing against me like it was trying to escape out into the world. As it crested into a deafening noise, the otherworldly whisper cut through it all with one word:

Awaken!

My hand brought the microphone to my lips and I heard my voice shout into the darkness.

"Maidensong harmony power...go live!"

The song exploded like a rose blooming, a tidal wave of warmth and euphoria that consumed every fiber of my being. It felt like the world itself was enveloping me in a cocoon of softness, shielding me from all pain and fear. The intensity of it all was startling, but I welcomed it with open arms, reveling in the overwhelming surge of raw power coursing through me.

I felt the ground disappear beneath my feet and realized I was floating. My limbs moved in slow, graceful arcs, guided by the song. With each turn, I felt my body changing, transforming into something new.

My clothes strained against my skin in unfamiliar ways, revealing curves and contours that were not there before, as a bold, radiant glow began to emanate from me. I held my breath, feeling the song's need to escape, pushing against the inside of my heart.

And I realized that I *wanted it to.* All doubt had gone, and I knew then that I wanted to shine.

Permission granted, the song's glow burst out, splitting into vibrant hues of purple that enveloped me and added speed to my twirls. As I spun, my clothes faded away, and I watched as a new outfit began to materialize on my body.

The warmth from the energy pulsed outward from my heart, creating a visible wave that rippled across my skin. In its wake, a black jacket with dazzling purple trim appeared on my torso. At my waist, an angled black skirt took shape, longer in the back, with matching purple trim.

The glow faded, and the new boots on my feet slammed onto the pavement with a solid jolt. The final note of the song reverberated inside me, filling me with unwavering confidence and determination.

And the voice returned, echoing in my mind once more.

You are reborn, my maiden. Now, save her.

Without question or hesitation, I understood. As time returned to normal, I ran toward my target, dimly aware that I was running faster than I ever could have before.

I leapt over the creature carrying the dumpster, landing between it and Nova. As the creature raised the dumpster above its head to crush us, I let out a ferocious cry and launched into a spinning kick that connected hard with the creature's head. It was thrown backward, tumbling over itself as the dumpster flew out into the street in a thunderous crash.

Nova must have turned around, because I heard her stammer behind me.

"Keyboards, are you—"

I stared at the creature I'd just kicked, pointed at it, and felt words pass from my lips from somewhere deep inside, the final words of the song of my rebirth.

"I am a guardian of song and heart! Servants of the darkness, be silenced by the song of Riot Purple!"

In the breath after, all doubt finally erased, I turned to face Nova, her megawatt smile almost blinding.

"I knew it!" she shouted. "I flammin' knew it! You're a maiden, babe! Get a look at yourself!"

I stared back at her in a mixture of disbelief and joy. "What happened to me?"

Nova slid her phone out of her jacket pocket and opened the camera app. She held the screen up to my face, and I saw myself for the first time.

My costume highlighted curves on my chest and hips that I'd always wished for but never thought I'd have. The skirt flared out around shapely legs in knee-high boots. My hair cascaded down to my shoulders, framing a face that was recognizably mine, but soft and rounded—I even dared to think *cute*.

Nova beamed and pointed at the screen. "You were closeted, babe! And now you're a grade-A certified magical girl!"

I couldn't believe what I was seeing or what Nova was saying, but as I looked at myself on the screen, a sense of euphoria washed over me. I was no longer hiding who I truly was, and it felt liberating. The magic inside of me had finally been unlocked, and I was ready to embrace it fully.

The creatures were regrouping for another attack. Shoulder to shoulder, tensed like coiled springs, we stared them down as they approached. The power in me was telling me to fight, slipping past my anxiety, and I couldn't deny it. I didn't *want* to deny it.

"You ready to do this?" I asked.

Nova shot me a wicked grin. "You better believe I am! You won't have a weapon yet, but you'll do fine! Lemme help ya with crowd control, and let's get in there!" She swung her fists in a series of mock uppercuts.

I nodded, not sure what I was agreeing to. If Nova had a strategy, she wasn't forthcoming. I felt around in my mind for something that seemed right. "Um, I guess you give me an opening?"

Nova raised her glowing drumsticks. "I got ya, babe! Get ready to move!"

With a small nod, Nova summoned her holo-drums drums and played a beat, another song I knew from the band's setlist. I listened for a moment, felt the rhythm pumping in my chest, and rushed toward the nearest creature.

She executed a thunderous fill on the drums, and a glowing circle of blue energy appeared beneath the creature. Within that circle, shockwaves ripped into it from all sides, and the creature recoiled as the waves engulfed it. Taking advantage of its disorientation, I moved in time to the beat, slipped between the shockwaves, and rammed my fist as hard as I could into the creature's face.

My punch reacted with Nova's energy, and I smashed the creature up against one of her shockwaves. I saw the creature's shell discolor as fissures formed across it and realized that if I kept to Nova's rhythm, I had all the power I needed. I punched it over and over in time with her beat, and our combined attacks pummeled it back and forth until a chunk of the shimmering white shell flew off. Thick black goo spilled out of the hole in its body, and it screamed and reeled back from me.

By this point, the second creature was getting closer. I turned my attention to it just in time to see Nova come flying in, feet first, and slam into its chest. She rolled and leapt back to her feet as her target dropped to the pavement, and I took my opportunity. I ran over and brought both my fists down on its shell, knocking a hole in it, spilling more of the foul-smelling black goo. It sizzled as it made contact with the pavement.

The first creature had struggled back to its feet and came at us again, far more unsteadily than before. I could see pulsating tubes and sacs in the hole I'd punched in it.

"I think we're 'bout ready for a final blow, Purple," Nova said. "You in?"

I smiled at the mention of my new color. "I'm in, Blue."

She beamed at me. "Then feel my rhythm and take the solo, babe!"

I sprinted toward the creature. It pulled back one of its spike arms with the clear intention of spearing me, and I let it think it might actually pull that off until the last possible moment. Just as it heaved that spike at me, I dove down and hurled myself toward its legs. I slammed into them and sent the creature tumbling down over me, and I hit the pavement. With a final push, I launched myself back up and skidded to a stop, then rushed the creature again and grabbed hold of it from behind.

Though I couldn't understand the creature's sounds, it definitely seemed surprised, and that was before Nova leapt at it. She held her arm up as she flew at the creature, and a glowing cymbal materialized in her hand. She brought the cymbal down on the creature's head with massive force, and another bright flash of blue energy blasted it upon impact.

The cymbal cratered into the creature's shell and punched straight through. It fell slack in my grip before it burned away into a cloud of blue particles that dissipated on the breeze.

Nova kept going and changed course. She ran at the other creature and hurled the cymbal out of her hand, sending it slicing straight into the hole in the creature's chest. It screamed before it, too, disintegrated into a cloud of blue particles.

Nova stood there and caught her breath, then gestured her hand at the cymbal now lying on the pavement. It rose into the air a few feet, took on a blue glow, and de-materialized.

Then, she turned back to me, grinned, and patted me on the back.

"Flam! Purple, you're so cool! You really pulled it off! I wish everybody else coulda seen it!"

I smiled back and tried to respond. Instead, I felt my limbs go weak, and I stumbled back, barely keeping my footing.

Nova grabbed my arm and tried to steady me.

"Purple? Babe? Hey, you alright? Stay with me, okay? Hang on, the crew's almost here!"

It was no use. My vision cartwheeled, hazy with purple energy. I felt myself changing again, as if partially returning to my old form. I regained awareness just in time to see the sidewalk rushing up at me before everything went black.

| 3 |

I came to, glad to find I was no longer on the sidewalk. I was sore all over, and my vision was blurry. I blinked slowly, tried to bring the room into focus, and decided I must be in a hospital.

If it was a hospital, though, it wasn't like any I'd been in before. I glanced around; the room was sleek and minimalist and metallic, and behind the bed I lay in, an array of glowing displays looked more like something out of a sci-fi movie, though judging by the CRT monitor that displayed my vital signs, it was a movie made in the early 1980s.

With some effort—and less pain than I expected—I propped myself up on my elbows and took a look down at my body. Even beneath my gown and the bed sheets, I could tell that the physical changes I'd experienced last night had mostly stuck, but I could feel them fading.

I definitely did not enjoy that sensation.

A soft chime sounded, and I heard footsteps. Moments later, a middle-aged Hispanic woman with a kind face and a lab coat appeared above me.

"You gave us all a scare," she said. "Don't be alarmed, okay? Just relax and save your strength."

I nodded and eased myself back against my pillow. "Where am I?"

"If I told you that you were in an underground facility a hundred feet below Old Town, would you believe me?"

That should have seemed impossible, but after what had happened with Nova and those creatures, I had no idea what impossible meant anymore.

"I guess I'd believe that, sure," I said. "I think I fought aliens or something before I woke up here. An underground bunker's not that big a surprise."

"You've still got your memories. That's good!" She laughed. "The aliens don't look like that, though."

"What?"

She smiled. "Would you like to sit up?"

"Um, okay, sure, yeah. Who are you, anyway?"

"My name's Marisol," she said as she pushed a button on the side of the bed and raised the part under my back to a gentle angle. "Dr. Marisol Barrera. How's that feel?"

"Good, yeah. There's a doctor a hundred feet below Old Town?"

"That's one of the hats I wear, yes. Doctor, medical researcher, paranormal xenobiologist..."

I shifted in the bed and groaned a little as I took some weight off a sore spot. "You're making that last one up."

"That's funny to hear, coming out of a magical girl."

Things began to snap into better focus in my brain. "So, all that stuff was real."

"Oh, sweetie, it was very real. I have to say, considering you went through an unexpected awakening, extensive magica feminization, and immediate engagement with the Pandora Corruption, you did an amazing job adapting to the situation."

"An unexpected... what?"

She raised her left wrist, and spoke into the same kind of watch-like device that I'd seen Nova wearing. "She's ready for you."

"*Got it. We're on our way,*" said a voice from her wrist device.

She leaned in closer to me. "Speaking of names, what can we call you? I don't mean the name I saw on your ID. I mean the name you want to have."

I froze. I had, of course, thought about what name I'd pick if I ever came out, but since I'd convinced myself I wasn't good enough to actually do so, I'd never told anybody. Not even Hazel, and she was my best friend. I'd always thought it was something I'd live with in secret for the rest of my life. A dream in the form of a cloud of vapor that would dissipate if I reached for it.

"How do you know about that?" I asked.

"I've worked before with trans girls who came out of the closet when they awakened. You don't have to be afraid here, sweetie. You're among friends."

I felt a warm sensation in my chest. I'd thought about this for a very long time, and actually getting to say it out loud was more of a thrill than I had prepared for.

"In that case—I always wanted to be Claire. Claire Ryland."

She smiled at me, a smile that managed to lower my anxiety just a bit further. "It's very nice to meet you, Claire. I look forward to getting to know you."

The door on the far wall of the room slid open, and in walked the members of Magica Riot. Sara led the way, with Cass and Hana close behind, and Nova bringing up the rear. It was hard to believe they were just here, in the flesh; only a short time ago, meeting all of them would have been the wildest thing that had happened to me. Now, it wasn't even in the top ten.

Before they reached me, Dr. Barrera stood and intercepted them and told them something in a voice barely above a whisper, which was met with nods from the group. She then stepped away, turning her attention to another bank of glowing displays, and the band made their way over to me.

"So, you're Claire," Sara said.

I laughed, giddy from hearing that being used to address me. "I'm not used to hearing that name out loud, but, um, yeah, I guess I am."

"It's a great name," Hana said, "and it's lovely to meet you, Claire! This probably wasn't how you wanted to meet the band, huh?"

"Gotta be some crazy revelations for you," Cass said.

The fight with those weird creatures was coming back into focus through my mental fog, and none of those memories were helping make sense of things.

Monsters in Portland. My favorite band being magical girls. Magical girls existing.

Me being a magical girl.

"I'm not sure which part is the craziest, to be honest," I said.

Nova slipped past the rest of the group and placed her hand on my arm, wearing the same enormous grin I remembered from the bar. "Well, I love the name, babe. It rolls off the tongue so much better than Keyboards! Plus, it suits you. Claire, Claire, Claire! My friend Claire!"

I had no idea how she could maintain that hyper-charged cheerfulness after what had happened to us.

"Friends, huh? I like that."

"Nova here makes friends real fast," Cass said.

Sara frowned. "Sometimes a little *too* fast. What happened to you last night, Claire, was not how we like to handle these kinds of things."

"Uh, well," Nova laughed nervously, "what's done is done! I mighta gone a *little* outside the rules, but sometimes ya gotta get out there and grab the girlies by the hand as soon as ya see them! You're here now, so it was worth it!"

I looked around the room in search of a clock, but didn't see one. "Hey, how long was I out, anyway?"

"Almost twelve hours," Sara said as she offered me a restrained smile. "How about we take a walk? Dr. Barrera says you should be okay to get on your feet again."

"Okay. Where to?"

"Just around the Vault. Might as well give you the tour. We'll wait outside while you get ready."

With that, they shuffled out of the room, Nova waving back at me as the door closed.

I got out of bed and retrieved my clothes, which, of course, fit noticeably differently on my altered frame. I may not have been quite as curvaceous as I'd been immediately after my transformation, but I was definitely not back in boy-mode, either. The warmth and sense of correctness I'd experienced was still there, too.

Uplifted but still confused, I left the room and entered a metallic hallway leading off into the distance, with various other doors leading to rooms branching off from there. The scale of the place was surprising, and I kept coming back to what Dr. Barrera had told me.

"So, this place is beneath Old Town? How did this get built with nobody noticing?"

"They built it when they did the MAX trains back in the eighties," Cass said.

"Okay, but like, who built it? The government? Are you working for the CIA? FBI? Military?"

Cass laughed. "We don't have anything to do with the government."

"The Portland Vault is owned by the Starlight Alliance," Sara said.

I stared back, perplexed. "Owned by the what-in-the-hell, now?"

"Watch the language, babe," Nova said.

"The Starlight Alliance," Sara repeated. "When you have hundreds of magical girls all around the world, it becomes beneficial to have an organization to manage them all. That's what the Alliance does."

"The whole thing's a big secret," Nova said, "and we don't have anything to do with governments or any of that stuff."

I shook my head. *"Hundreds* of magical girls?"

"It's not really that many, when you think of the size of the planet," Cass said.

"That's not the part I'm hung up on."

Hana giggled. "This takes me back! Oh, Claire, there's so much for you to learn!"

"It sure seems like it. It's just hard to believe all of this is here in Portland."

"The Pacific Northwest is actually a hotbed for magical girl activity, and everything related to it," Sara said. "The Cascade range is heavily infused with thaumatite."

"That's the crystals that channel magica," Hana helpfully added.

"Yeah," Cass said. "Lots of magical girl stuff up here. The Vault used to be busier. You should have seen it three, four years back."

"Why's that?" I asked.

Sara frowned, ever so slightly. "That's not important right—"

We were interrupted when one of the doors we were passing, with large block lettering above it that read ARMORY, slid open. A very animated muscular redheaded woman with a noticeable Irish accent stalked out of it, making a beeline for Nova.

"Now you hold it right there, Miss Nova," the woman said. "You can't hide from me all day."

"Saoirse, hey," Nova said as she brought her hands up to a defensive stance. "What's up, babe?"

"You sent those new cymbals flying into the shell of a Pandora, didn't you?"

"And they worked great!"

"They ain't designed for that, you spanner! Your kit's made for support use in Riot mode, not assault! That little stunt left microfractures in the alloy. How are you going to feel when you pull them out of the aether next time, and they disintegrate?"

Sara motioned toward the woman. "Claire, if you haven't figured it out yet, this is our most recent addition. Saoirse O'Carolan, the armorer of Alliance Portland. Saoirse, this is Claire Ryland."

I waved, not wanting to draw her fury. "Hi."

"Hey," Saoirse said. "So, you the new keyboard player?"

I flinched. This was new information, and for a moment, I was more anxious about joining Magica Riot *the band* than I was of getting skewered by monsters. "Um, what?"

Sara shot her a disapproving look. "We haven't talked about that."

Saoirse nodded. "Better do that, then. I gotta get back to work. Lots on my plate."

With that, she turned and walked off into her armory.

I looked back to the rest of the band. "New keyboard player? What was she talking about?"

Sara motioned for me to follow in the direction of another door marked TRAINING. "I guess it's time for us to have a talk, in private."

We entered a large room made of flawless, shining white panels from its floor to its surprisingly tall ceiling, bathed in uniform light. The place looked big enough to put on a sizable concert, but was completely featureless except for a small touchscreen mounted by the door. The air in the room was oddly still and quiet, as though there was a lot of soundproofing behind those glistening walls.

"What is this place?" I asked.

"Every band's gotta have a practice space," Cass said.

"It's also a nice, quiet place to chat," Sara said. "I realize this is all a lot to take in at once. You seem to be handling the first bit of it pretty well, though."

"The first bit," I said. "You mean—"

Nova grinned and gestured toward my body. "Being a girl, of course!"

I looked down at myself again. Though I felt comfortable in this new form, it was still hard to believe it was real. "That's something I've wanted for a long time," I said quietly.

"I know how you feel, babe! It was the same for me!"

"You came out because of all this, too?"

"My awakening happened a little bit after I came out, but that's just details. Gettin' a giant dose of magical hormones was just what I needed to go all-in! That first time is so good. I betcha you're startin' to feel it wearing off, though, ain't ya?"

I nodded, not trying to hide my disappointment. "Yeah. It's like I felt totally *right* inside, and now there's a little hollowness. Maybe that's what I felt before and never noticed. Either way, I don't like it."

"Sounds familiar! We'll get ya on the regular non-magic stuff to balance it all out, and you'll be feelin' good again!"

My shoulders relaxed in relief. "Thanks. So then, this song thing—"

"Only a very small percentage of women of all kinds have a connection to the Maidensong," Sara said. "As the voice says, those who carry the pure heart of a maiden are called by it."

"Why did it choose me? What made me so special?"

"The song finds girls on the edge of a change," Cass said, "ready to help people. The job of magical girls is defending the innocent and the powerless against, well, you got a taste last night."

Sara walked over to the touchscreen on the wall and tapped a few buttons. Suddenly, one of the creatures we'd fought downtown appeared out of thin air in front of me, looming as tall and terrifying as the ones last night. The shimmering shell, empty black eyes, and needle-sharp spiked arms were unmistakable.

My heart raced and my mouth went dry. I tensed, ready to dive out of the way of an attack. It took me a moment to realize that the creature was completely motionless.

"It's okay," Sara said. "This is just part of our training software."

"Good instincts, though," Cass added.

The creature's image flickered, and I relaxed a bit. The sight of the thing still tweaked something in the back of my mind, an echo of the feelings I'd experienced while fighting them. For all my confusion at everything that had been dropped on me in the last twelve hours, some newly awakened part of me knew how dangerous these beings were—and more importantly, that I was meant to fight them.

"What *are* these things?" I asked.

"This," Sara said, "is just one of countless threats that magical girls face. Some of them come from this planet, some come from others, and some—like our friend here—come from places we've got no words to accurately describe."

"You probably figured out by now that we don't really know much about them," Cass said. "They're not even from our dimension."

Hana nodded. "It's quite a mystery! We've got amazing researchers, but it's a complicated problem to crack."

Sara continued. "These creatures have been traced at least as far back as the Pandora myth, which is why we call them the Pandora Corruption, for lack of a better name."

The name was vaguely familiar, but history had never been my strongest subject. "The Pandora myth?"

"The Greek lady who opened up a box and let evil out into the world," Hana said. "These might be the source of that myth! It's really fascinating."

I looked over the creature's hulking body again. I had a natural tendency to avoid putting myself in harm's way, to just stay out of the spotlight and try my best to avoid being perceived. Now, I had a new world opening up in front of me where none of that was possible, but the sensation of correctness and strength I experienced last night was far too enticing to deny, even if I still had no real idea what was going on.

"So, what do you want with me?" I finally asked.

The four of them raised their arms into the air and those now familiar glittering microphones materialized in their hands. They brought the mics down to their mouths and recited the phrase I'd used the night before.

"Maidensong harmony power ... go live!"

Moments later, the room sparkled with hues of red, yellow, green, and blue. The feeling in the back of my mind grew stronger as my skin was bathed in the warmth of the light.

Gradually, the energy faded, and the four of them stood before me. With them all together, I saw for the first time their coordinated look as a team. All wore the same costume: the jackets, the skirts that were longer in back than in front, the boots, and gloves. Where Nova's costume had blue panels and accents, the others had their own associated color. Red for Sara, yellow for Cass, green for Hana.

"You know us as a band," Sara said, "but that's only part of the story. We are the guardians of song and heart, a magical girl band protecting the innocent through the power of music and kindness."

"Riot Blue," Nova said.

"Riot Green," Hana said.

Cass nodded. "Riot Yellow."

"And Riot Red," Sara said. "We are Magica Riot, and we've decided that we want you to join us, Claire Ryland."

I hesitated. Somewhere inside me, a voice screamed for me to accept, to change my world and jump in with both feet. All I had to do was say yes, and my life would be altered forever. And I realized with surprise that all the years of who I *had* been, the entirety of what I'd called a life, only barely stacked up to equal this new voice.

I also noticed I hadn't said no yet.

"Do you really think I'm cut out to do this?"

"Babe, I was there last night," Nova said. "You are a magical girl, no doubt!"

"We've all learned and improved as we went along, and it's made us stronger as people, and as a team," Hana said.

"I know you felt what we all feel," Cass said. "The power. The confidence. Don't let your pre-awakening nerves take that away from you."

"Besides," Nova continued, "I think it was meant to be! You play keyboards, babe! You showing up and turning out to be a maiden ... it's like everything's turning around for us!"

Sara stepped closer to me and reached out her hand. "Nova said you called yourself Riot Purple. That name means something to us." She paused; the entire room seemed to hold its breath. Finally, she added, "So the choice is yours."

Already, as I stood there in the group's presence, those anxious feelings were starting to dull. The sensation of warmth and joy I'd experienced the night before had returned in full force, and it was urging me forward. All I had to do was open my heart.

And that's when I heard the song again.

Instinctively, I raised my arm and felt the weight of the crystalline purple microphone materialize in my hand. I lowered it to my mouth and recited the transformation phrase.

The same purple light filled my vision, and I rose from the floor, slowly twirling as the energy flowed over me, replacing my old clothes with my black and purple outfit. When the light dissipated, and my feet returned to the floor, I was renewed.

I felt, once again, completely correct in my own skin.

"Okay. I'm honored to be your new Riot Purple."

Sara took my hand and gave it a firm shake. "Welcome to the team, Claire."

Nova looked by now like she was about to burst, and she dove and glomped onto me with a surprisingly forceful hug.

"I'm so ready for this! It's gonna be so much flammin' fun to have you around, babe!"

I laughed and hugged her back, then paused; a fresh anxiety popped into my head, and I felt cold dread creep over me.

"I'm not going to have to sing, am I? I'm not really sure how I feel about my voice, and—"

"Don't worry about that," Cass said. "You can focus on playing, it's totally fine."

I sighed in quiet relief. "Okay, cool. So, what happens next?"

Light emanated from the four of them again as they de-transformed, and Sara motioned for the door.

"Let's go make this official. You still need to meet the commander."

| 4 |

"The commander" turned out to be a tall, solid mountain of a woman named Meredith McCoy who looked to be in her forties. Behind her glasses, she had the tough, weatherbeaten features of someone who'd spent most of her time outside around horses and old pickup trucks. Her graying blonde hair was gathered up into a simple ponytail, and she talked with the steady drawl of a rancher. Looking at her, I felt oddly homesick; she reminded me of the kind of tough women I knew in my old hometown, back in rural Texas.

My impression of her was correct, as the framed newspaper clipping sitting proudly on her desk revealed she actually *had* been a rancher who'd organized efforts to stop a fascist group from setting up shop in her hometown in southern Oregon. And now, she was watching over me with a broad smile on her face as I tapped through an agreement on a tablet officially making me a member of Magica Riot and the Starlight Alliance, while the rest of the band waited outside her office.

I paused at the signature line. "So, do I put my legal name, or the name I've been using here?"

Commander McCoy gave the tablet a glance through the bottoms of her bifocals. "As far as that goes, just sign it as Claire. We'll handle everything for you."

I smiled and completed the form before passing the tablet back to her. "Okay, done."

She glanced down at the screen and nodded. "Then that's that. Welcome to the team, Agent Ryland."

"I'm excited to be here," I said. Which was true, but I figured I didn't need to let on about all my additional anxiety to the woman in charge of the whole thing.

"Just know, you don't have to put on a front," she said, as if she could see right through me. "I know this here's a big deal. You've got a million questions, and we don't have all the answers. S'okay to be nervous."

I let out a small sigh of relief. "Yeah, I'm scared, too. I don't want to get killed by monsters. But the excitement's a lot stronger."

She leaned across the desk and took my hands. Hers were strong and calloused, but she held mine gently. "I wish I could tell you this is easy. Alliance Portland's a little less put-together than it used to be, and we're all wearing a dozen different hats here. Y'all have to make some of this stuff up as you go, figure out your own path. You girls have more power than anybody can imagine. As long as you use your power responsibly, for the good of those that's weaker than you, you'll do great."

I nodded back at her. "I'll try my very best."

"I know you will," she said, as she pushed back from the desk and stood. "The Maidensong wouldn't have found you if you weren't ready to be a hero. For now, though, go home, get some sleep, and get ready for training. The band's got a show coming up next month, and I'd love to see you join them."

The prospect was more than a bit daunting, but exhilarating all the same, and I couldn't help but grin. "Sounds good. I'll be ready."

"Oh, and Claire?"

"Yes, commander?"

"Don't forget to pick up your hormones from Dr. Barrera on the way out."

"Right, yeah, that's important. Thanks."

She winked and gave me a nod. "Anytime."

I stood and walked out through the commander's office door to find the rest of the band, along with Dr. Barrera and Saoirse, waiting for me.

"How's it feel to be official?" Cass asked.

"Good," I said. "Really good. A little terrifying, too, but good."

"Welcome to the team, new girl," Saoirse said. "Just don't take too much advice from Miss Nova and you'll do fine."

"Hey, c'mon, lay off," Nova said. "I'm practically Claire's big sis!"

"You're four years younger than her!"

Dr. Barrera gave me a trio of pill bottles. "Spironolactone, estradiol, and progesterone. Take one spiro in the morning, one prog at bedtime, and one estradiol four times a day. And welcome aboard!"

"Thanks," I said. "I'll try to remember it all."

She chuckled as she handed me one more item. "I'll email you the instructions. Also, you left your phone in the medical bay."

With everything that had happened, I'd completely forgotten about my phone—and when I tapped the wake button, I was greeted by a screen full of text messages from Hazel, asking if I was okay with increasing concern.

I felt like a fool. Of *course* she'd be wondering what happened to me. And now, I'd worried her. What if she thought I was dead? Or I was blowing her off and ignoring her? Maybe this is how our friendship would end: her thinking I'm a callous, distant jerk, and me watching as she left me forever. My heart pounded harder as I considered all the ways my neglect could doom me.

"Oh, uh, I need to go," I said.

"Everything okay?" Sara asked.

"Yeah, for sure. I just need to make sure my best friend knows I'm still alive."

* * *

Video Frenzy was a sprawling independent video rental shop in an old building out on Southeast Belmont Street. It held a special place in my life because it's where I'd made my closest friend since I moved to Portland.

Hazel Hoffman seemed purpose-built to spend her days surrounded by stacks of 35mm film cameras, old bootleg tokusatsu VHS tapes, and dusty boxes of obscure vinyl records, the kind of girl whose closet seemed to be stocked entirely with flannel and jeans. I thought she was basically the coolest human being I'd ever known, and for some reason, she didn't mind having me around, so things had worked out well between us.

I spotted her as soon as I entered, re-shelving box sets in the sci-fi section. Fortunately, there were no other employees nearby, which would make concealing my newly feminized form easier. I hunched a bit to try to take attention away from my chest, but there was nothing I could do about my hair.

As I approached, she noticed me, and the relief on her face was obvious.

"Hey! You're alive!"

"Yeah," I said. "I'm so sorry, Haze. I didn't mean to worry you. My phone died."

She reached up and brushed her shaggy blonde hair from in front of her green eyes. "It's okay! I was just a little worried. Honestly, I didn't expect to see you today. Figured you'd be recuperating after the show."

My mind flashed back to Dr. Barrera and the medical bay. "Yeah, uh, I definitely was. I really crashed."

"I hear that! Magica Riot shows can really take it out of you."

I laughed nervously. "You can say that again."

She started to say something, but stopped herself, and looked at me curiously. "Hey, are you okay? You look kinda ... different. It's like you're—"

I felt myself blushing and glanced around to make sure nobody else was in earshot. "Actually, Haze, I really need to talk to you. Some, uh, stuff has happened. You have a minute?"

"Sure, yeah, I can take a break," she said as she continued to eye me suspiciously. "You wanna go up on the roof?"

A ladder at the back of the building led up to Video Frenzy's rooftop, and the employees kept a few lawn chairs and a mini-fridge up there for break purposes. As I sat in one of the chairs, Hazel pulled back the tarp that protected the fridge from rain and rummaged through the contents inside.

"Couple of peach sours in here. You want?"

"Sure, yeah," I nodded.

She reached into the fridge and pulled out two bottles, holding them with their necks in-between her fingers. Then, she stood and walked over to the wall around the edge of the roof. With a single fluid motion, she whacked the edge of the caps down against the top of the wall and popped them off.

I'd seen her do that so many times now, and I still had no idea how she pulled it off.

She handed one to me. I took a long sip.

"Thanks."

"Always! So, you gonna tell me what's up?"

I had to be careful how I handled things, so as not to accidentally reveal my magical secret. I decided to approach it from the gender side first.

"Do you ever look at me and think I could be something else?"

She cocked an eyebrow and thought for a moment. "What, you mean like employment-wise? Or are we talking about something bigger?"

"Well, things have happened to me in the last day." I paused, and laughed, as it hit me that not even twenty-four hours had passed since my awakening. "Anyway, it's kinda uncorked a bunch of feelings I've had bottled up."

"This have something to do with your hair, and, y'know, *those?*" she asked, gesturing at my chest.

My breath caught in my throat. Admitting this to the band had been one thing—they were involved with it, after all—but telling Hazel would be opening up a raw part of myself I'd buried for most of my life. Not that I expected her to react poorly, but the vulnerability was very present.

I wrung my hands together, suddenly feeling like I was back in elementary school about to explain a bad grade.

"So, um, what would you say if I told you that I was ... a girl?"

She nodded, took a sip of beer, and smiled at me, warmly and genuinely.

"I would say that I'm glad I'm friends with such a kind and sensitive girl."

I felt a blast of joy in my chest. "For real?"

"Of course! I ain't a piece of shit."

"I know you aren't! I didn't mean to say that you—"

She laughed and reached out to touch my shoulder. "Relax. I believe you when you tell me who you are. Plus, it *does* explain some things about your whole vibe. I always thought of you as an honorary lady, and now you're official!"

I'd never felt tears well up in my eyes so quickly. "That's one of the nicest things you've ever said to me, Haze."

"Well, it's true. Trust me! I'm a lesbian. I know women. I love women." She leaned in closer. "What do you want me to call you now?"

"Claire," I said, as much a statement of purpose as a simple declaration. It felt more right every time I said it.

"Nice," Hazel said. She looked up and gestured with her free hand toward the sky. "Claire Ryland. I love it! God, that's a pretty name." She returned her attention to me and nodded confidently. "It suits you."

Suddenly, my cheeks felt hot. I looked down at my beer. "Aw, thanks."

I had never experienced *that* sensation when Hazel and I talked before, but I did still like girls; transition hadn't changed that. My newly recalibrated hormones were apparently doing a number on me.

Hazel sat back in her chair and took a deep drink from her bottle. "So! You have any more life-changing revelations today?"

I laughed. "Well, I joined a band, too."

She sat back up, grabbed my arm, and leaned in close as an expression of raw shock grew on her face. I had never seen her move so quickly.

"Excuse me?"

"Yeah," I said, trying to remain somewhat calm in the crosshairs of her intensity. "Um, you're looking at the new keyboard player of Magica Riot?"

Hazel looked as if she might combust. "Get out! You joined *Magica Riot*? How did that even happen?"

I shook my head. "It's a surprise for me, too. I guess we just really hit it off last night at the show. Sara Ward herself made me the offer." All of that was, technically, in a roundabout way, completely true.

Hazel shook her head, leaned back in her chair, and slammed the rest of her beer before turning back to me. "This is more of a surprise than you being a girl. You know that, right? Magica Riot! That's incredible."

I sat back and nodded. *If only I could tell her.*

"Believe me, Haze, you don't know the half of it."

| 5 |

My first month as a magical girl passed in a constant rush of band practice and combat training. I had an entire back-catalog of songs to practice before I had to play a show, as well as the small matter of learning how to fight monsters from beyond time and space without getting killed. These activities were roughly equal in terms of stress.

We practiced song after song, over and over, nearly every day. When band practice would end, magical girl practice would begin, and we'd run different scenarios in the training room against holographic enemies as I began to get a grip on my musical weapon: a keytar.

Keytars turned out to be very flexible weapons, bridging the gap between long-distance and up-close fighting. I'd play mine in rehearsals and fight with it in combat practice. When the day was over, Saoirse took the keytar back and did *something*, and the next day, I'd use it some more. This process of tweaking and refinement went on, but I was never told the specifics.

Nor was I told exactly how to handle a magical keytar. Sara said something once about it being important for me to "feel it out for myself," but she didn't explain what she meant by that. And so, I tried my best. My early attempts at fighting were awkward and fumbling, but I'd started to find my footing. I also learned the different ways the band communicated while fighting, shouting codes like "bridge" and "big finale" that were connected to improvised plans and attacks.

This routine continued until we'd reached the day before my first gig with the band. After we wrapped combat training, Saoirse walked into the training room, took my keytar, and then motioned for us to follow her.

"C'mon now, it's time we see if you're proper settled."

"Proper ... what?" I asked.

Sara shut off the training program and wiped the sweat from her brow. "You think it's ready?"

"Aye, that it is," Saoirse said as she slowly rotated the instrument in her hands. "The keytar's absorbed a lot of her—" she gestured vaguely at me "—bio-essences ... and such." She turned to me with a satisfied look on her face. "And you, new girl, you've been really suckin' diesel lately."

I glanced at the rest of the girls, looking for a clue. "Is that good?"

"She means you've been making a lot of progress," Hana giggled. "Take it as a compliment!"

I was so used to Saoirse's bluntness that receiving praise from her hit doubly hard and I felt my cheeks get warm. "Oh, um, well ... thanks."

Nova walked up and rested her arm on my shoulder. "Heck yeah, babe! That means we gotta see if you and the keytar are bound now!"

"Bound? What does that mean?"

"The final step of learning to wield magica-powered weapons," Sara said. "You'll see."

* * *

Of all the facilities I'd spent time in at the Vault over the last month, the armory still felt the most mysterious. An array of large, serious-looking computerized lockboxes with bulletproof glass windows lined the far wall. Some were empty, and some held instruments I'd never seen anybody use. The rest of Saoirse's equipment looked like hybrids of regular tools and magical implements, the functions of which I could never guess.

This time, to my surprise, the room also contained Dr. Barrera and Commander McCoy.

"Thanks for meeting us," Saoirse said to them as we entered. "I think the day's finally come."

Dr. Barrera shot me a smile. "Our girls grow up so fast. I'm so proud of you, Claire."

"Um, thank you," I said. "What for?"

"If what Saoirse says is true," Commander McCoy said, "you and your keytar have a real relationship now."

I couldn't hide my confusion. "A relationship? You're talking like it's a person."

"Naw, I wouldn't go that far. From what the girls tell me, I'd say it's more like a horse."

"Claire," Sara said, "you've felt it by now, haven't you? How your instrument feels less like a tool, and more like a participant. A partner, even."

I paused for a moment, and thought. Truth be told, I *had* been feeling something as I used the keytar. Every time we'd practiced, it felt more capable, in a way that went beyond my own increasing skills. It almost seemed, when magica was surging through it in the heat of combat, that the keytar itself was helping to channel my abilities.

"Well, I guess I have," I said. "I didn't know exactly what was happening, though. Nobody explained anything to me."

Sara sighed and nodded. "I'm sorry about that. It's part of the process. It's important that you and your instrument form a relationship that's your own, free from outside influence."

"I still don't get it. Are you saying these things are alive?"

"There's not really a simple answer for that."

Hana stood beside me, placed a hand on my shoulder, and gestured out in front of us, as if she were gazing at a grand vista. "Think about it like this! It's magica. 'Life' is too small a concept here. Magica itself is a life force. It flows from life, through the universe, and into things like the thaumatite crystals in our instruments, or ourselves, as magical girls. The instruments have a kind of life, because magic is part of life!"

"Aye, that's a good way to look at it," Saoirse said as she slipped on a set of goggles and laid my keytar onto her workbench. "My master armorer back at Tokyo HQ always called it 'the resonance,' the way magica comes alive in thaumatite and magical girls. Sympathetic cosmic frequencies, and what have you."

She unbolted a panel on the back of the keytar and removed it to reveal a glimmering, crystalline structure embedded in a piece of circuitry so futuristic and complicated-looking that I couldn't even begin to make sense of it.

"Let's see what we've got here," she continued as she tapped a button on the side of her goggles. They extended like zoom lenses on a camera, and she leaned in close to the crystals, studying them intently. "Good growth structure here." She glanced up at a nearby computer display filled with numbers and graphs. "Strong energy profile. I'd say this keytar likes you, Miss Claire."

"Oh, that's good," I said. "So, what now?"

"I think it's best that a magical girl take over here," Saoirse said.

Sara nodded to her and stepped toward me. "Go ahead and transform."

"Okay," I said. I focused on the Maidensong. My microphone materialized in my hand, and I recited the transformation phrase.

"Maidensong harmony power … go live!"

The room lit up with purple energy, and a few moments later, I stood there in magical girl form.

"Alright," Sara continued, "think about your instrument and reach out for it. Not here, in the room. If you're bound to it now, you'll feel it somewhere in your mind. Find it, and pull it through from there to you. Got it?"

I did not get it at all.

"Uh, sure," I lied. "I'll give it a try."

I closed my eyes and focused on the keytar. Right away, I sensed something, a magical presence in some other place. I zeroed in on it, and it grew stronger. The image of the keytar began to form and solidify in my mind, until I felt a magical jolt. My eyes opened just in time to see the keytar disappearing from the workbench and materializing against my chest, its strap already across my shoulder. It took form, solidified, and I immediately felt its weight.

"Wow. Okay, that's really cool."

Cass grinned at me. "Right? Never gets old."

"Now that you're bound to it," Sara said, "you can dismiss it to the aethereal plane and retrieve it at any time."

"Aye, and what's more, no one else on Earth can use it now," Saoirse added.

"Little safety feature," Nova said. "Sweet, huh?"

"Makes sense," I said. "Alright, what now?"

Sara gave me a smile, a *noticeable* smile, the first I'd ever seen from her. "Now, we get ready for the gig tomorrow night."

* * *

The following evening, we met up at the Vault and made our way down the main corridor to a room I hadn't been to before, at the far end of the facility. I looked up at faded lettering above the door reading VEHICLE STORAGE.

"Vehicles? Do we have some kind of flashy combat cars, or giant robots, or something?"

"Nothing like that," Sara said.

Cass laughed. "Not even close."

Hana clapped her hands and smiled at me. "I'm so excited! You get to meet the last member of the band!"

"I don't follow," I said.

"Babe, it's a special night," Nova beamed. "You finally get to meet Vancent!"

Sara opened the door and led us into a garage that, like the medical bay, looked like the set of a movie that would have been impossibly futuristic in 1980. Multiple racks of bulky CRT monitors and dusty collections of sci-fi power tools lined walls in front of faded paint stripes delineating parking spaces. Like everything in the Vault, the room was large, but it now held only a single vehicle.

A dark gray early '90s extended-length Dodge van.

"Claire," Sara said, "this is Vancent Price."

"That is not what I expected," I said, staring at the van and trying to figure out what I was missing.

"Vancent's been here since before Magica Riot even existed," Cass said. "He's a real warrior."

Hana nodded. "In a way, he's the most senior employee of Alliance Portland! He was transportation for the last three generations of Portland magical girls."

"Miracle Bridge, The Roses, even Jade Evergreen herself," Sara said. "Vancent's been here for all of them."

Nova reached over and gave me a squeeze. "All the real legends! This van's got tons of history, babe! And now, you get to be part of it!"

I walked over and opened the double doors on Vancent's side. Unlike every band van I'd seen before, Vancent was immaculate.

His gunmetal gray paint was glossy and smooth. The interior, with its four rows of bench seats, was covered in what I could only describe as "bordello red" cloth and carpet, top to bottom. The seats were plush and springy. He even smelled nice. The most unusual thing about him was how normal and non-magical he seemed.

"This is actually a really nice van," I said, "though I'm kind of surprised there's not any magical girl stuff in here."

"Vancent's got a secret identity, just like us," Sara said. "He's been carefully designed to look like a conventional van, but under the skin, he's basically a mobile extension of the Vault itself."

"And extremely tough," Hana added. "This van's been through a lot over the years."

"The Alliance might have taken a bunch of the Vault's equipment when they relocated staff to Seattle and San Fran, but they're never gonna take Vancent from us," Cass said.

I looked at everybody else. Their reverence for this old van was obvious, and I could feel it rubbing off on me already.

"Well then, I'm really glad to meet him. I have to know, though—why was he named Vancent Price?"

"Nobody remembers," Nova said. "He's just always been Vancent Price."

"If The Roses named him, I bet a lot of beer was involved," Cass said.

Sara chuckled. "That's probably a very safe bet."

| 6 |

As the evening light faded, we pulled up to the stage door in the alley behind the venue. Cosmic Club was an older bar in the ground floor of a building on the Central Eastside. I'd seen several bands play there. It had great vibes, all wood paneling and mid-century light fixtures, and a friendly staff, though people always said the owner was a bit of an ass.

Sara shifted Vancent Price into park and turned around in her seat to face the rest of us.

"Okay, we're on at ten tonight. So far, the sensor grid's been quiet. Nothing out of the ordinary. Still, let's keep our ears and eyes open. Claire, how's your link working for you?"

I looked down at the device on my wrist, identical to the ones worn by the rest of the band. "It's good. I think I'm getting my head around it."

"Great. Since this is your first time, let's just try and relax and have fun. Doesn't look like it'll be a packed house tonight, so remember, no pressure."

"Right. Got it."

"Cass, Nova," she continued, "take a walk through the crowd before we start and get a sense of things. If you pick up any weird vibes, let's make a note of them. We could have more Pandora grunts disguised as people."

"You got it, boss," Cass said.

"Heck yeah," Nova said, "none of those creeps are gettin' past us!"

"Great," Sara said. "Hana, you still up for working the merch table tonight?"

Hana nodded. "I'll merchandise like none have merchandised before."

"Alright. Let's load in. Hopefully, tonight will be nice and calm."

We managed to get our amps and other gear up on the stage before the bit of an ass made himself known.

"Well now, if it ain't Portland's washed-up prima donnas, gracin' my stage with their presence again!"

The five of us looked down at the smirking face and spectacularly unpleasant demeanor of a fifty-something man in a reproduction Metallica T-shirt and pre-ripped jeans that probably cost more than my monthly grocery budget.

Sara snarled more than she spoke. "Artie. What a surprise to see you here."

Artie placed his hands on his hips and laughed. "It's my club, ain't it?"

"Usually, you're too busy crashing Porsches to care what folks are doing with their leisure time," Cass said.

"Pretty high-and-mighty for a band that don't finish their sets half the time," Artie spat back. "You're lucky I got more respect for my booking contracts than you do for business."

"Well then, you should be happy for us to fail," Hana said. "If we crash and burn, you won't have to see us again."

"We ain't gonna, though," Nova quickly added, "so you're just gonna have to get used to us!" She seemed genuinely agitated.

Artie scoffed. "Big talk." He finally noticed me, and stared at me as he tried to figure out if I belonged there. "Who are they? New roadie?"

"*She* is our new keyboard player," Sara snapped.

I tried my best to remain out of Artie's spotlight. "Um, hi."

He stared at me for a moment longer, and then seemed to decide I was of little concern. "Whatever. I don't care how big your egos are. You could go save the world for all I care. When you're at my club, on my stage, you're just another act, and you better give me at least thirty minutes of music. Got it?"

"Oh, anything for you, Artie," Cass snarked back.

Artie shook his head, spun on his fancy sneakers, and walked off to spread his mood poison somewhere else.

Sara sighed once he was out of earshot. "I'd rather fight a hundred Pandoras than deal with Artie Duncan."

"He definitely seems like an ass," I said.

Nova shot me a look. "Language, babe!"

Fortunately, we had no more encounters of the Artie kind as we set up. Just as I was getting everything plugged in for my amp, a familiar voice from off stage caught my attention.

"Hey, rock star!"

I turned just in time to see an old film camera snap my photo.

"Gwhaaaa," I yelped in confusion. The photographer giggled.

"Pure perfection," said Hazel. "That one's going in my portfolio!"

I could already feel myself starting to blush, and I tried my best to remain calm. "You didn't have to work tonight?"

"I traded shifts," Hazel said. "It's not every day your best friend makes her stage debut, is it?"

"Aw, well, I'm really glad you came."

Hazel grinned up at me. "You really do look like a rock star up there, you know? I'm so proud of you!"

From her drum kit, Nova called out to me. "Hey Claire, who's that?"

I glanced back to find that the rest of the girls were all looking at Hazel and me.

"Well, everybody, this is my best friend—"

"I think I know you, actually," Hana said. "I've seen you at shows before!"

"Yeah, me too," Cass said. "Uh, Hazel, right?"

Hazel's eyes widened. "That's right, yeah!"

"Oh yeah, I remember you, too," Sara said. "It's good to see you again. You've come to a lot of our gigs."

Nova, of course, would not settle for mere talk. She leapt over her drum kit and dove toward the edge of the stage, somehow managing to hang off the edge far enough to give Hazel a hug without falling onto the club floor.

"Flam yeah, it's good seeing you again! I totally didn't know you and Claire were tight. Any bestie of my bestie Claire is a bestie of mine!"

Hazel laughed as best she could while Nova squeezed the air from her. "Thanks! I didn't think y'all would even remember me. Never expected *this!*"

"Yeah," I said, "I should have told you. Nova is a hugger."

Hazel eventually pried herself from Nova and headed off to get a beer. I turned back to the stage, as the rest of the girls stood directly in front of me with various sizes of grins on their faces.

Nova poked me in the chest. "Best friend, huh?"

"Best friend," I said. "Yes. Best friend."

"Such very good friends," Hana said with a giggle.

"Uh-huh," Cass said. "I also got blushy and awkward around my best friends, right before I started dating them."

I felt the heat in my face reach critical levels. "What? I wasn't awkward."

"You were pretty awkward," Sara said. "In a cute way."

"I was not awkward," I protested.

Cass continued. "Claire, you *like* like that girl, don't you? You wanna—"

"Alright, alright," Sara said, "let's give her a break. People are showing up. Let's just relax and get ready to perform."

Suddenly, our wrist links lit up with a call from Commander McCoy. We moved off to the back of the stage and huddled up before answering.

"We're here, Commander," Sara said. "What's up?"

Commander McCoy's voice sprang out of the link. "Agent Ward, we're getting some readings on the city sensors. Two signatures. One's low-level Pandora activity. The other's something else."

"Something else? Like what? The Spectarians? Bio-mechs?" Sara's voiced lowered. "Has Sorceress Makula coalesced?"

"No ident yet. It's weak, but it ain't a false reading. Keep your eyes open."

Sara looked around at the rest of us and frowned. "Acknowledged. Ward out."

"Well, that didn't sound encouraging," Cass said.

"No, it didn't," Sara said. "Be alert."

"Bio-mechs?" I stammered.

Hana put her hand on my shoulder and gave me a sympathetic expression. "We'll get you Epsilon clearance soon."

* * *

As the house lights dimmed, we walked out onto the stage. Even in the dark, I could see the people out there in the crowd, waiting and watching. Some started to clap and shout for us, and for a moment, I froze in anxiety.

This was really happening. No turning back now.

My mouth went dry, and I felt my hands start to tremble. If I screwed this up, I could hurt the band even more than they already were, and the prospect made my stomach churn.

Cass, who was nearest to me on stage, must have picked up on my fear. She reached over very subtly and touched my arm, and as

I looked away from the audience toward her, she smiled at me and spoke gently and quietly. "You okay? You got this?"

I took a deep breath and nodded back at her, then reached down and powered on my keytar. One way or another, I was going to make it through.

The stage lights snapped on with a *pop*, bathing us in a rainbow. I could hear the air near the bulbs sizzle. Just at the edge of my vision as I tried to adapt to the lights, I caught sight of Hazel, front and center, right up next to the stage with her camera to her eye, and I felt the blush return to my cheeks.

Sara stepped up to the microphone as she put her fingers on her guitar's fretboard. "Hey, friends. Thanks for coming. We're Magica Riot."

Another, louder cheer went up from the crowd, and Nova began counting out the beat of "Second Promise, Second Chance." My breath caught in my throat; the song had opened the band's first album without Iris, and I felt the weight of it being the song that began my time with them.

Our music blasted out of the amps, and I was swamped with sound and punched by the thump of Nova's drum kit. For as exciting as it was to listen to the band from the crowd, being up on stage was a thousand times as energizing, and I felt my heart pumping as I started to play.

Sweat was already beading up on my forehead. I was a little shaky at first, despite all of the practicing, but by the end of the first chorus, I could feel myself entering the groove.

It did feel a bit like I was riding a wild animal that I had no control over, but at least I was starting to enjoy the ride.

So, of course, that was the moment it all came crashing down.

A tremendous *bang* shot through the room from somewhere outside. Every single light fixture in the club burst in a shower of sparks, plunging the room into darkness. Our amps all powered off, our performance replaced by shouts and surprised screams from the crowd.

"Oh, come on," Cass said. "Really?"

Moments later, the emergency exit lights came up, and the head bartender shouted out across the room.

"Everybody, please stay calm! We lost power. There's no danger! We're looking at the problem. Just hang out for now."

Sara turned around and shook her head. "Of all the nights for this to happen. Let's stay put and see if—"

The night took another swerve as our wrist links lit up again. We huddled together once more as Sara opened the channel.

"Commander? Do you have an update?"

"*Alert status. Six Pandora Corruption signatures and the unknown energy readings, within two blocks of Cosmic Club. Intercept and engage, transformation approved.*"

Sara sighed. "Copy that, commander. On our way."

"*Good luck, Magica Riot. McCoy out.*"

Our links went dark again. I exchanged glances with the rest of the band.

Cass let out a long, low whistle. "Six, huh? Busy night."

"Better than dealing with Artie," Hana said.

I took a deep breath, then exhaled. "This is the real deal, huh?"

"As real as it gets," Sara said.

"Heck yeah, let's do it to it," Nova grinned. "Time to kick some butt, magical girl style!"

We headed toward the stage door, only to be intercepted by Hazel.

"Ugh, I can't believe there was a blackout tonight, of all nights," she mourned. "You all sounded so good!"

"I know, right?" Hana said. "We'll get it next time."

"They might get the power back on soon," Hazel said. "You could still finish!"

"It's probably gonna take time," Cass said. "We need to step out back for a few."

"Oh, okay," Hazel said. "You want me to come find you if they fix it? I could—"

"We'll be fine," Sara said. She seemed to realize she'd been blunt, and her expression softened. "We've got to have a band meeting about the situation."

"Right, yeah," Hazel said. "I get ya. I'll be hanging out, so come find me when you're done!"

"We will," Sara smiled. "Be right back."

As the other girls followed Sara out the back door, Hazel stopped me, concern evident on her face.

"Claire, is everything okay? Seems like a weird time for a band meeting."

My heart thumped. "Oh, yeah, totally! We just hadn't expected this. Sara wanted to talk about our plans, that's all."

Hazel nodded. "What about you? Are you okay?"

"Uh, what do you mean?"

She looked at me quizzically. "Your debut got interrupted before you finished the first song. It's totally okay if you're sad about that."

Right. My brain was already shifting into "fighting monsters" mode, so I'd pushed my disappointment down inside me for now.

I nodded. "Oh, yeah, I mean, of course. It sucks, but it's not our fault, so I'm just trying to roll with it."

"Yeah, I hear ya," she said. "I guess being in a band's kind of a different life, a different mindset. I'm proud of you for keeping your chin up."

My face felt warm. "Aw, thanks, Haze."

She smiled. "Okay, go have your band meeting. Come back soon, rock star."

"I will," I said. "Just wait here, okay?"

"Yeah, I ain't going anywhere," she said. "You sure everything's okay?"

I nodded in the most convincing way I could manage. "Everything's going to be fine."

If we were lucky, I might even be correct about that.

| 7 |

We slipped out the back door of Cosmic Club into the alley and immediately spotted the source of the power outage: a burning transformer atop a power pole next to the building.

"Pretty interesting timing, don't you think?" Cass asked.

"Interesting, yes," Sara said. She glanced down at her wrist link's scanner and pointed down the street in the opposite direction. "This way. Let's go."

Unfortunately, we weren't the only people who had stepped outside.

"Just where do you think you're going?" Artie stood farther down the alley, engulfed in a cloud of cigarette smoke.

"Show's over," Sara said. "Haven't you noticed?"

"Oh no, you aren't bailing on me again. Get back on that stage, and—"

Sara turned and pointed up at the flaming power pole. "Then fix your stupid electricity, Artie!"

Nova stuck out her tongue and blew a raspberry in Artie's direction as Sara motioned for us to follow. We took off down the street as Artie's complaints faded in the distance.

"To be fair," Hana said, "the transformer was probably the Pandora Corruption's fault, yeah? We're all thinking it."

"I'm not going to give him even a little satisfaction," Sara said.

Guided by Sara's wrist link, we zeroed in on the Pandora Corruption signals. As we got closer, my heartbeat started to quicken, and my hands trembled. It wasn't as though I had never fought Pandora monsters before, but that first time, I had the benefit of ignorance and adrenaline on my side. Now, I knew exactly what was waiting for me, not to mention the pressure of doing a good job with the full team for the first time.

I tried to calm myself with a deep breath, but my nerves were beyond easy help at that point.

We turned a corner onto a dark side street that was enclosed by the walls of the tall, old brick buildings that made up so much of the inner southeast side of town. The street was oddly quiet, despite being in the middle of the city on a Friday night. Slowly, as my eyes adjusted to the darkness, I spotted the source of the energy readings we'd followed, and it chilled me.

Mid-block, three people huddled together against the wall of a building, surrounded by six humanoid figures, spaced in a mathematically even semi-circle around them. Despite the distance, I could see the generic blankness on their faces. They advanced, tightening the semi-circle with inhuman precision.

"There's our targets," Sara said. She looked back at the rest of us. "Suggestions?"

Cass studied the scene for a moment. "Half of us could go around through the alley over there and escort the civilians away while the other half distracts the Pandoras."

"Or we could make a lot of noise, fake a fight between us, and draw their attention," Hana said.

Sara nodded. "Solid ideas. Claire?"

I froze in full deer-in-headlights mode. "Um, well, I think, for sure, uh, either of those."

Nova grinned and shook her head. "I dunno what we're all standin' around yappin' for when there's a real easy thing we could do!" She advanced toward the Pandora creatures, grabbed a rock laying against the curb, and hurled it at them from the hip with near-perfect little league outfielder form.

The rock smacked one of the creatures squarely in the back of the head with a dull *thwump*, and slowly, all six of them turned away from the civilians to face us, that familiar empty malice on their faces.

Cass sighed. "Yeah, that's also an option, I guess."

"How could we forget the Nova method?" Hana giggled.

Sara cupped her hands to her mouth and called out to the trio of civilians "Are you folks okay over there?"

A bearded twenty-something in a flannel shirt shouted back. "They're trying to mug us or something!"

"We'll take care of them," Sara said as the five of us started to close the distance. "You folks need to get out of here, right now."

"I don't understand," flannel guy said. "What's going on? Who are you?"

"We're professionals," Cass said.

"For real! You gotta scram," Nova said.

Flannel guy stared at us for a moment in confusion before relenting. "Yeah, okay, okay. Thank you, whoever you are."

He and his companions slipped past the creatures and took off running down the street. One of the creatures turned to follow.

"No, no, no," Cass shouted. "You're dealing with us now!"

As if in reply, the creatures returned their attention to us, and began to emerge from their human disguises. The same agonizing ripping and snapping sounds I remembered from my first night came back, as their false skin tore apart and peeled off. Their hulking forms swelled up from inside, dislodging gore and flesh that slid down and plopped off onto the pavement. In the dim ambient light, their chromatic shells gleamed, wet with the fluid of their transformation.

I felt that distant sensation in the back of my mind again, the recognition of an ancient evil and my duty to oppose it. That feeling smashed headlong into my fear and anxiety, and I tensed.

"Looks like we won't be talking this out," Cass said.

"It's time we went to work," Sara said. "Let's go!"

As I tried to push aside my fear, I raised my hand into the air alongside the rest of the girls. Our crystalline microphones appeared in our grasp, and we brought them to our lips as we opened ourselves to the song.

"Maidensong harmony power ... go live!"

The darkened street lit up in rainbow colors as we lifted off the ground, our bodies outstretched and gently twirling as the energy of the song coursed through us. Our street clothes vanished as our costumes materialized. I returned to the ground as the warmth of transformation washed over me, nourishing my core while the rainbow peaked and subsided.

When it was over, we stood side in the face of the approaching Pandora creatures.

"We are the guardians of song and heart," Sara said as she stared them down and pointed at them. "Servants of the darkness, be silenced by the song of Magica Riot!"

The Pandora creatures, now fully transformed, stared back for a moment before rushing forward. Their spiked arms pulled back to pierce us as they closed the remaining distance with terrifying speed.

"Scatter and regroup!" Sara shouted as her guitar materialized in front of her.

Cass nodded. "Going wide! Gonna try and draw a couple out of the crowd!" She leapt to the right and rolled out of the path of the creatures as they advanced.

I dove to the side, feeling a breeze as a Pandora spike sliced past my face. I heard Sara playing the first chords of "Second Promise,

Second Chance" and tried to count off the beat as I dodged the attack.

Sweat beaded on my forehead and my heart pounded, the fear and the thrill mixing into a potent fuel. My leg pushed off the pavement, and I rolled and sprung back up to my feet.

Behind me, the creature had flown past and stumbled, but regained its footing. I spun to face it. As I'd practiced, I reached out to my keytar with my mind and felt the weight of it materialize against my chest.

The creature turned toward me. I played the song's riff and aimed at its center mass. With a crackling *zap*, a bolt of magical energy flew out of the keytar.

My aim was slightly off, and it glanced off the creature's shell, which only seemed to irritate it.

Again. I played and fired. This shot hit home, and the creature roared and snarled, but kept advancing at me. Its shell was scorched and scarred where I'd hit it. A clear, viscous fluid streaked with oily black goo weeped from the wound.

Again. Another shot. Another scream. *Again. Again.*

The power of the Maidensong rippled through me. That sensation of boundless ability, a drug of confidence, coursed along my veins and nerves. I felt I could do anything. I *would* do anything. I was a guardian, a maiden, a being of immense potential aching to be unleashed against forces that would harm the innocent. I would be their protector.

I thought all of this, right up to the moment when I felt the arm of another creature slam into my torso.

The impact flung me through the air like a rag doll until I was stopped by the brick wall of a building. I slammed into the wall with a hard *thud* that rattled my organs and knocked the breath from my lungs. Dust and rough chunks of brick flew off the wall, and I fell, unceremoniously smacking the sidewalk face-first. I felt the soft insides of my body rattle against my ribcage, radiating pain like a cold starburst. The adrenaline went sour in my stomach.

I groaned and started to force myself up off the pavement. I hurt from head to toe, but I was still alive, and the magical girl side of me knew I had to get back into the fight.

Before I could stand, the creature reached me and beat me down again with the side of its spike arms. The one I'd shot quickly joined in the assault. I tried to roll away, but their pummeling was relentless.

One of them tried to jab their spikes into me, but I jerked to the side and it missed, its arm crunching into the sidewalk instead. It tried again, and I dodged at the last moment. I was getting lucky, but I knew that luck would run out.

I hadn't paid attention to my surroundings, and because of that mistake, I was in serious trouble.

The blows kept coming. I felt like I was being tenderized. Fortunately, I had enough mobility to keep dodging the spike attacks, but I wasn't sure how long I could hold out. I caught glimpses of Sara and Cass, locked in combat with the other four creatures.

Where were Hana and Nova? Were they—

A glowing blue circle of energy appeared beneath the first creature and thumped upward in time with the music, knocking it off-balance. The second creature had no time to react as a translucent green shockwave bulldozed into its body and hurled it against the building.

I was so rattled I didn't realize what was happening until I saw Hana and Nova's faces looking down at me.

"It's dangerous to go off by yourself," Hana said. "Always take your rhythm section!" She cracked a grin.

Nova reached down and took my hand. "This is a real moment! You just got your butt kicked for the first time!"

Hana took my other hand, and the two of them hauled me back up onto my feet.

"It's a magical girl rite of passage," Hana said. She patted my back and then stopped to slam the body of her bass down into the nearest creature as it struggled to stand. "You're lucky you stayed conscious!"

I tried to refocus. "Ugh, I'm sore."

Nova grabbed the second creature and heaved it into the street. She gestured to it as if presenting it as a prize on a game show. "Shake it off, babe! Let's smash these jerkos!"

"We'll give you the rhythm," Hana said, slipping her bass strap back over her shoulder. "See if you pick up what we're laying down!"

She and Nova started to play again, falling back onto the beat as if they hadn't missed a single moment of the song. I listened for a moment, locked eyes with Hana as she thumped out her bass line, and joined in with my keyboard part.

Hana smiled and nodded to me, and her part started to diverge. Her fingers slid and danced across her bass strings, leaping across the fretboard. She added complexity and tones that weren't in the song before, improvising a new part that fit with mine in a completely different way.

I felt a connection there between my keytar and Hana's bass. Magica surged between us, and my keytar resonated louder and stronger inside than I'd felt before.

She was boosting me for another attack.

I turned, aimed, and fired a bolt of magica at the more distant creature, a shot more pointed and forceful than any I'd loosed before. It sliced the air and jackhammered the creature's shell with a ferocity that pierced straight through and blasted out its back. The chitin cracked with loud snaps that reverberated off the nearby walls, and a breath later, in a spray of shell fragments and black goo, the creature dropped to the pavement and dissolved into a mist of purple energy.

Hana switched back to playing her usual bass part, and with the last remnants of the overdriven magica in my keytar, I spun around and smashed the neck of my keytar down into the other creature's shell as it tried to get up again. I finished my riff and shot a magica blast into it, and the creature's insides, superheated by the magica from my strike, exploded outward, sizzling as it hit the walls and pavement.

"Wow," I said, "that really works."

"I can't do it too much," Hana said. "It takes most of my power, so I need Blue to stabilize me, but it can give us a real edge!"

Nova grinned. "Pretty cool, right? Now let's go help the others!"

Out in the street, Sara and Cass were in intense combat with the four remaining Pandora creatures. This was my first time seeing them in a real fight; Cass stayed back, using shots from her guitar to harass the monsters from a distance, giving Sara openings to slice and smash them up close. She and Cass fought in unison. Cass was precise and methodical, and Sara slipped out of her usual restraint and became ferocious, a fiery whirlwind of attacks and parries and dodges.

Artists in battle, as on the stage.

"Blue, let's hit them with a disorientation spell," Hana said, "and give Purple an opening to attack."

"Heck yeah, babe," Nova said. "I'm ready!"

I felt my words choke up in my throat. "Won't I get in the way?"

"We believe in you," Hana said. "You've got the keytar. You can cover the distance!"

She and Nova switched up their playing again, and rippling shockwaves roiled out across the street and smacked the remaining creatures. The effect was instantaneous; their attacks became less coordinated, and their movements slowed.

This time, I watched before I acted. I noticed where Cass was focusing her fire while Sara fought in the mob, and a plan formed in my head. And with Hana and Nova watching my back, I might be able to pull it off.

I listened and matched Cass's guitar riff as best I could, and sensed magica coursing through the keytar again. The power grew more and more intense and fed back into me. I could feel what Saoirse had said before, about the resonance. The keytar thrummed with the energy of life and filled me with a wave of strength and confidence.

Now, it was time to ride that wave.

I aimed at the nearest creature and fired. A searing, intense bolt of magica lanced through the air and blasted the creature in the back of the head, burning a scorched wound into its shell. It screamed, a moist and guttural sound, and turned around in confusion, which took more attention off Sara.

That was my opening. I let go of my anxiety and embraced the Maidensong, and started running. My boots pounded the street as I hurled myself into the fight. As I neared the creatures, I switched to playing chords, re-charging the keytar and sharpening its body for close combat. Magica tingled and vibrated through me, and the Pandora creatures got closer and closer, until they filled my vision.

I swung the keytar and smashed it into the first creature's body as I pushed into the fight.

The creature staggered, and I ran past it toward the second, jabbing the neck of the keytar into its back. This caught it by surprise, and it tried to spin to attack me. I dove under its arm and landed hard on my right leg. My muscles burned, but I shoved off, jumped back to my feet, and spun around, landing back-to-back with Sara.

"Nice moves," she said. "Glad to see you on your feet again."

"Good to *be* on my feet," I said. "I really screwed up at first."

"It's growing pains. We've all been there. You get back on the bike and keep going."

I nodded. "You got it."

She nudged me with her shoulder. "Follow my lead, Riot Purple."

Her body tensed, and as magica flowed into and between us, I understood what she had planned. I readied myself, and a moment later, we acted.

Sara's intent was clear, and I followed in her wake. She sang and moved in a dance of fury and strength. Holding it by the neck, she swung her axe-like guitar in smooth, connected arcs, relentlessly slicing into the Pandora creatures. I felt her flow and synced with it, cutting into the creatures from the other direction. The sound of gargling roars and shattering chitin came from every direction as we spun and dodged through the pack, sending globs of their otherworldly fluids flying to the pavement. The creatures tried to fight back, but we slipped past their attacks with inches to spare.

And there, in the heat of the fight, I felt something new.

The magica in my keytar swelled higher, the strongest I had ever felt, and the energy in my body resonated to match. The power that pumped through me felt nearly limitless—and then, suddenly, I hit a limit, a wall. It was the strangest sensation, as if there were incredible, endless heights beyond me, but something was blocking me from them, purposely holding me back. No matter how hard I pushed, I was stopped.

The sensation lasted only a moment, but it was unmistakable. And, unfortunately, distracting.

As Sara and I reached the fourth and final Pandora creature, I misjudged my attack. My keytar swung through open air next to the creature, which threw me off-balance. My feet snagged on each other, and I stumbled straight into the creature's counterattack.

Its arm smashed into my chest, and I screamed and started to fall. The pavement rushed up at me, but the impact never came; a heartbeat passed, and I felt Sara's strong, muscular arm wrap around me and pull me up.

"I've got you!" she shouted. "Back on the bike!"

And then, without breaking her stride, she pulled me close. With a fluid pirouette, she twirled us around and slammed her guitar into the final creature's head. She hit it with such force that it buried itself deep, smashing through the shell.

Using our combined weight and momentum, she spun one more time and yanked the guitar up through the rest of the creature. Its head snapped from its body, the shell chitin ragged and shattered.

As we came to a stop, the previous three creatures staggered around behind us, their shells cracked and glistening with weeping fluid and black, slimy goo.

This was my chance to do something.

While Sara recomposed herself, panting and sweaty, I aimed my keytar at the remaining creatures and called out to Cass, Hana, and Nova.

"Big Finale!" I shouted. "One! Two! Three! *Four!*"

On the downbeat, the four of us rang out the final riffs and chords of the song, and blasts of magical energy leapt from our instruments and converged on the trio of badly injured Pandora creatures. Their shells succumbed to the blast, cracked and crumbled into a wet mess, and vaporized into a cloud of energy.

As quickly and violently as it had begun, it was over.

8

As the last of my strength faded, I slipped out of Sara's grasp and flopped onto my back on the pavement. I felt like I'd been run over by a series of trucks, but I was alive. Despite all the mistakes I made, that had to count for something.

Sara must have noticed my exhaustion, and she kneeled beside me. "Purple? You okay?"

"I think so," I said. "Just really sore. Unless I broke something and don't know it yet."

She shook her head. "That's unlikely. It takes a lot more than that to break a magical girl's bones."

"That's good," I said, happy for my bones. "What about the *rest* of a magical girl?"

Satisfied that I was not dying, Sara tapped her wrist link and opened a comm channel back to the Vault.

"Riot Red, reporting in. Six Pandora Corruption beings dispatched. We have some bruises, but no serious injuries apparent. Civilians not alerted."

"*Copy that, Riot Red,*" Commander McCoy's voice answered. "*Be advised, we no longer see Pandora signatures, but those other readings are still there.*"

Sara frowned. "Acknowledged. Can you clarify? Do you have a fix?"

"*Uh, they're right on top of you. Do y'all not see anything?*"

She looked around the empty street. "Negative, commander. No contacts visible. Please advise."

I laid my head back down on the pavement and gazed up at the sky, and that's when I saw them. A trio of silhouettes, six stories above us on the roof of a nearby building, barely visible against the glow of the city lights reflecting off passing clouds.

They seemed to stare down at us with three pairs of glowing red eyes.

I looked away, hoping that whatever they were, they hadn't noticed that I'd seen them. As subtly as I could, I reached up and touched Sara's arm, giving her sleeve a quick tug.

"Hey, uh, Red?"

"Stand by, commander," she said into her link as she looked down at me. "What's up?"

"I think I see them."

She nodded slowly. "Are we being watched?"

"Yeah. I saw three of them."

"Where are they?"

"Up on a rooftop, on the right," I said.

She pursed her lips, and sighed. "Alright. We have to catch them."

"How are we going to get up there?" I asked. "Can magical girls fly?"

"No, but we've got an alternative."

She looked up and motioned for the rest of the girls to join us. "Yellow, Green, Blue, I need your help over here!"

"What's up? Everything okay?" Cass asked as the three of them reached us and kneeled down around me.

Sara mimed helping me with an injury as she spoke. "Don't look, but we're being watched from the rooftops."

"Of course we are," Hana said. "Nothing's ever simple, is it?"

Cass shook her head. "The other contacts. What are we gonna do about them?"

"We need to get up there," Sara said. "Blue, I know it's been a while, but do you feel like pulling off a trampoline?"

Nova's eyes went wide and she laughed the most nervous laugh I'd ever heard from her. "Uh, yeah! Yeah, sure! That's, uh, totally a great idea to try again!"

"What does 'pulling off a trampoline' mean?" I asked.

"I can *sorta* bounce us off my drums," Nova said. The way she emphasized "sorta" implied it was doing a lot of heavy lifting.

"What she means is, we might not all land where we want," Cass said.

"I can do it," Nova stammered, "it's just not real precise, is all! I ain't exactly Neil Peart!"

"Regardless, we can't let those things get away," Sara continued. "Purple, you sit this out. You've already been through a lot tonight."

Despite my aches and pains, I felt like I could do it. Even though I'd made some mistakes tonight, I'd also felt a moment of real harmony in that fight. I wanted to take on the work, just like everybody else.

I looked up at Sara. "No, I'm in."

She stared back down at me, her expression serious. For a moment, she looked away, her frown deepening. Then, she exhaled, a sort of half-chuckle under her breath, and cracked a smile. "Alright. I'm going to count us in. Yellow, you go on the downbeat. Green, Purple, you go on the next bar. Blue and I will follow a bar later. Assuming you land on the roof successfully, start running. Chase them down. Tackle them, if you have to. Let's see if we can get some answers."

Cass nodded. "Right. Let's do it."

Nova turned around and called up her holo-drums. With both hands, she shoved them out away from her onto the pavement.

"One, two, three, *go!*" Sara shouted.

Cass leapt onto one of the drums and shot skyward. Hana grabbed me by the arm, yanked me up to my feet, and pulled me along with her. We jumped onto the second drum and flew up into the air, faster and more abruptly than I'd expected. We arced upward over the building and fell back down, landing in a hard roll on the rooftop.

My already-sore muscles screamed at me, but I pushed up and forced myself back to my feet. Ahead of me, I saw the mysterious silhouettes already running away, with Cass in hot pursuit, and took off after them as fast as I could.

Somewhere behind me, I heard Hana's footsteps and the sound of Sara and Nova smacking into the rooftop, followed by Sara's voice urging us forward.

"Keep going! Don't let them get away!"

My heart pounded and my legs burned as I pushed myself, the edge of the rooftop getting perilously close as I zeroed in on one of the unknowns and closed the distance. Ahead of me, Cass leapt at her own target. I had only a moment to act before I ran out of roof, so I shoved off with both legs and threw myself toward the closest shadow.

I had only a split second to process what happened next.

The shadowy figure ahead of me spun around and hurled a fist at me. It slammed into my chest with the kinetic violence of a car crash. An explosion of magica burst from the point of impact, and for the briefest moment, I could see my attacker clearly.

It was a girl.

She might have been around my age, but a metallic mask framing her eyes made it hard to tell. Her grin, lined by black lipstick, curled cruelly as she struck me. I saw the ruffles of her black corset dress shake as her fist made contact, the impact shaking loose strands of her straight, violet hair.

I had just been punched by another magical girl.

I gasped for air as I left the rooftop and shot through the air, tumbling over and over, getting brief glimpses of city streets and buildings passing by beneath me.

Then, suddenly, I crashed through something wooden and slammed hard into a very solid surface, and the world went dim around me.

* * *

Eventually, I heard footsteps approaching, followed by voices.

"Purple?" Nova asked. "Purple? Babe? Oh no, oh no, babe, are you okay? Say something!"

"Purple, can you hear me?" Cass asked. "Can you move?"

I forced my eyes open. Nova was on her knees beside me, holding my hand, her cheeks streaked with messy tears. Cass kneeled on my other side and checked my pulse; nearby, Hana stood by Sara with her hand on her shoulder.

Sara stared, not at me, but through me. When I made eye contact with her, she shifted her gaze away.

I looked around and didn't recognize my surroundings, but it looked like a construction site. Above me, a hole punched down through shattered lumber and drywall indicated how I'd arrived here.

"Yeah, I'm alive," I said.

"Thank goodness," Hana said. Sara exhaled in relief.

Nova laughed even as she cried. "You can't do that ever again, okay?"

"You had us worried," Cass said. "They hit as hard as we do."

I pushed myself up by my elbows and realized I was at the bottom of a shallow crater in cracked concrete, the dust turning my costume to a dull gray.

"What happened?" I asked. "Where am I?'

"This half-finished apartment building was kind enough to catch you," Hana said.

"What about the other girls? Did they get away?"

Sara walked over and extended a hand to help me up. "They did get away, and we need to talk about them."

Unsteadily at first, I stood, Sara and Nova keeping me upright. Sara placed her other hand on my shoulder, squeezed it, and gave me a small smile and a nod.

"What did you see?" Sara asked.

"I only got a look for a second, but they looked like magical girls to me."

Sara sighed. "That's what Yellow said, too. And that's a problem. If they're magical girls that the Alliance doesn't know about, and they don't show up as magical girls on the sensors..."

"Then what are they?" Cass asked.

"I ain't never heard of magical girls fightin' other magical girls," Nova said.

"Me neither," Hana said. "It'd be the first time I'm aware of."

"Maybe they're something else in disguise," I said. "Like, monsters, or, I don't know, aliens."

"I doubt it," Sara said. "The aliens don't look like that. In any case, this is serious. We're going to need to make a report to the commander. The Alliance needs to know."

Once we were back to our regular forms, we returned to Cosmic Club. The flaming power transformer had been put out, and an electric company crew was on the scene working on it. Artie was out there, too, arguing with one of the crew, so we slipped past without attracting his ire.

Vancent Price was right where we'd parked him. Beside him, looking around the street, was Hazel.

She called out to us as we approached. "Hey, there you are! Welcome back! How was your ..." As she got a better look at us, she trailed off and her mouth fell slack. "Uh, are y'all okay? You look like you got hit by a truck."

"We had our meeting," Sara said, "and, you see—"

"I fell," I said. "Just tripped and hit the sidewalk kinda hard. That's all."

"You fell?" Hazel considered this for a moment and gave me a sympathetic look. "Aw, you poor thing. Come on in, and I'll buy y'all a round! The bartender's put out some candles, and she's still serving."

"We really need to be getting out of here," Sara said.

"Oh, I don't know," Cass said. "We could spare a few minutes. We still have to pack up our amps, and it'd be a shame to cut out so quick after the gig fell apart." She shot an insistent look at Sara. "Don't you think? Might be good for our image, and I'd hate to disappoint a fan."

Sara glanced at Hazel and her expression softened. "Well, you've got a point. Alright. Everybody, go on in. I just need to make a call."

Hazel grinned and clapped her hands. "Awesome! C'mon, the drinks aren't getting any colder."

The bartender was operating surprisingly quickly in these unusual circumstances, and I took several long sips of beer as soon as I sat down. Every part of my body hurt, though I now knew I'd have been in much worse condition if I hadn't been a magical girl. Exhausted, not just physically but in my soul, like I'd cried myself dry, I sequestered myself on a bar stool, hoping nobody would talk to me.

Off to my side, Hazel was having a bit of a fangirl moment, getting to hang out so casually with Magica Riot. She was busy talking about music with Cass, Hana, and Nova, who reveled in her can of Shasta cola like it was the last on Earth. Hazel looked lost in reverie, so I occupied myself with my beer, and my thoughts.

I was so lost in my own head that I didn't even realize Sara had returned and was sitting on the stool next to me until she nudged my arm.

"You okay?" she asked.

I looked up from my beer and offered her a weak smile. "Yeah. I'm okay. Tired. Sore."

"Maybe a little self-conscious?"

I winced a bit; she was on target, as always. "How did you know that?"

She took a sip of her beer and nodded slowly. "It's your first time. I know how it goes."

"Yeah," I said. I looked back down into the bubbles in my beer. "I'm sorry about my screwups. I really don't want to let any of you down."

"Claire, you're not letting anybody down, and you've got nothing to apologize for. We're a team. We work together."

I looked up to protest. "Yeah, but I could have done that a lot—"

"Every one of us can always do something better." She looked at me with the same quiet confidence I knew from seeing her on stage. "It's like I said, you get back on the bike, and keep going."

"Yeah, I guess you're right," I said. "Still, I can't imagine I really lived up to Iris's example."

"Iris is—was—special," Sara said. She sighed, a sigh that felt like it held a hundred stories. "What she wasn't was perfect at being a magical girl on her first try."

"Really?"

She turned to face me. "Do you remember that big blackout downtown, five years ago?"

"For sure, yeah," I nodded. "It was all over the news."

"That was Iris, about a week after she'd awakened."

"Seriously?"

"Seriously," Sara laughed. "She always said 'I never leave a job half-finished, for better or worse,' and she meant it. Gosh, that night was a mess. We were all messes."

I did the mental math. "Five years ago. Wow, you were all so young."

"Just teenagers," Sara nodded. "Cass and Iris and I were eighteen. Hana was seventeen. Hell, Nova was just thirteen! Made our powers and emotions potent. In all the ways you can imagine."

I didn't feel better, exactly, but I did feel relieved. I smiled. "I appreciate the pep talk. You're good at this."

"Thanks. Guess it's part of the job." She paused to take another long sip of beer. "For what it's worth, Iris would be telling you the same thing. I wish you could have known her."

"I wish I could have, too. The way you talk about her, she sounds amazing."

"She was the most incredible woman I ever knew." She sighed again and her expression fell. "I loved her."

My breath caught in my throat. "Oh, Sara, I'm—I'm so sorry. I didn't know it was like that."

"It's okay. I'm learning how to let go." She looked at me and smiled softly. "I'm sure you have somebody like that in your life."

The beer in my system sloshed over the red plastic cups of my mind and sent them toppling. "Me? What? No, no, never have, can't, me? Like that? No."

Which was the moment Hazel clapped her hand down on my shoulder. I tensed like a prey animal.

"Hey you two," she said amiably, "What's going on at this end of the bar?"

"Uh, nothing," I said, "just normal talk. Talking normal. About normal things."

Hazel giggled in the painfully charming way she did after she'd had a few. "You okay? You sound a little tense."

"Yeah, Claire," Sara said, chewing on my name like a lioness. "You sound a little tense." She grinned ferally.

I shook my head, a bit more frantically than was called for. "No, no, I'm just, uh, tired and sore, is all."

"Aw, I bet," Hazel said. "Tonight probably took a lot out of you." She placed her beer on the bar top, reached out, and started rubbing my shoulders. "Here, this'll help."

I froze. My heart raced as her thumbs and fingers pressed into me. "I, uh ... oh wow ... uh, Haze, you totally don't—"

"Wow, you really *are* tense," Hazel murmured, her hands digging into my shoulders. I whimpered.

Sara chuckled and took another sip of beer. "Can't imagine why."

| 9 |

The next morning, I awoke in my apartment to the sound of my ringtone. I hesitated to move; my soreness was less intense than the night before, but it was still present, a dulling ache over my entire body.

I groggily fumbled for my phone and tapped the answer button. Hana's voice sprung from the earpiece.

"Good morning, Claire!"

"Hana? What's up? Is everything okay?"

"For sure! I was just thinking that maybe I'd get everybody together at my parents' restaurant for one of our band dinners tonight. You free?"

Without coffee in my system, the question threw me off-kilter. "Your parents have a restaurant?"

"Totally! Hasegawa Fusion, on Dekum. Sound good?"

"Sure, sounds good."

"Yay! Alright, see you at seven! Bring an appetite!"

"Will do. See you then."

The connection closed, and I flopped back over onto my pillow.

I had almost drifted off to sleep when the phone buzzed again and ripped me back to consciousness. This time, it was Hazel.

"Hey, rock star! Did I wake you?"

"Uh, no, I'm already out of bed," I lied. "What's up?"

"I gotta work tonight, but I was hoping I could get your help with something before then."

I suddenly felt more awake; a chance to help out Hazel was probably also a chance to hang out with Hazel. "Anything you want, Haze. I'm there."

"You're the best. Alright, meet me at the rose garden. Nine-thirty, maybe?"

"Okay, yeah. Nine-thirty."

"Awesome. Wear something cute. See you then!"

The call ended, and I rolled over and drowsily stretched. If I'd been more awake, I might have asked what she wanted, but whatever it was, I'd be …

And then, my eyes shot open, and my anxiety spiked.

Why had she told me to wear something cute??

* * *

My wardrobe had slowly been evolving since I'd come out, but there was one frontier I'd yet to cross, outside of my magical girl costume: dresses and skirts.

I'd bought a simple dress for my first gig with the band, in dark purple with pink floral patterns and a cute shape. My courage had faltered, and I didn't wear it to Cosmic Club. After Hazel had called, I'd forced myself to put it on, but I was *not* used to wearing a dress in public; when I boarded the MAX, I became incredibly self-conscious and tried to avoid being perceived.

That would not be an option at the garden.

I got off the train and walked the rest of the way to the International Rose Test Garden, and—after a few moments of searching—found Hazel waiting for me on a bench, checking the settings on that well-worn old film camera she loved so much. As I got closer, she looked up and grinned at me and gave me a wave.

"Hey, rock star! You …" she trailed off, and her eyes widened.

"What, is something wrong?" I looked down at my outfit.

"No way," she said, smiling. "You just look really cute."

I blushed instantly. "Oh, um, th-thanks, Haze."

"I'm glad you came," she continued. "This wasn't gonna be any fun by myself."

"Oh yeah," I said, my head finally clearing. "What did you have planned that needed my help?"

She held up her camera. "I just got this new lens. Well, y'know, new to me. Fifty millimeter prime, one point two max aperture. Been waiting for ages to get one that didn't cost a ton, and then this one showed up at Blue Moon over in St. Johns. Still kinda pricey, considering it's from 1975, but she's a beauty."

I nodded. I didn't know what most of that meant, but I was excited for her all the same. "Cool! It looks nice."

"I know that all means jack to you," she laughed, "but the short version is it's got that creamy bokeh. Uh, out-of-focus parts, I mean. Anyway! I need to test it out."

"So you came to the rose garden. Makes sense. You need me for moral support?"

She grinned. "No, silly. I need you for a subject."

I froze. "Uh ... what?"

Hazel looked down. "I'm going to take photos of you," she said. Her voice was nearly a whisper. "In the garden."

My heart pounded. "Haze—"

"Yeah, I know. You always dodge the camera. You never even took selfies before you came out."

"Well, yeah. I mean, I didn't look right."

"You weren't you yet," she said. She was picking up steam again. "And now you don't have that excuse anymore!" She stood, smiled, and stared into me with those gorgeous green eyes. "You deserve to have some nice photos of you. Commemorate the official arrival of Claire Ryland, cool rocker chick."

This was not a development I had foreseen. Being perceived to this degree, getting photographed with a real camera—by

Hazel—was a little bit terrifying. And yet, I had no desire to turn her down. Funny, that.

"Um ... well ... what do you need me to do?" I asked.

She motioned for me to follow her. "I'll show you! C'mon."

We walked the rows of flowers until we reached some soft lavender roses that caught Hazel's eye. She leaned down close to them and took a deep breath of their scent.

"What do you think?"

"They're pretty," I said. "Kind of a citrus smell."

She smiled in a way that punched straight through to my heart. "Nice, huh? I think the purple is just perfect. It goes with your dress! Really suits you."

If only she knew the extent of my newfound connection to purple. "You think so?"

"Yeah! You'd look good with purple hair, actually."

"Aw, well, uh ... I'll have to remember that next time I hit the salon."

She grinned and gestured toward a spot on the ground. "So, I'd like you to stand here, and pose for me."

I walked over to where she indicated. "Okay. You know I don't know how to pose, right?"

"That's okay! I know what I'm looking for. Let me help. Is it okay if I touch you?"

My brain screamed. My mouth uttered mostly coherent consent. "Touch? Oh. Oh! Yeah! Okay! For sure! Whatever you need! Just put me wherever!"

Hazel's grin broadened into an amused smile. "Alright. Just put your feet here, to start."

I stood with my feet in the prescribed spots.

"Okay, cool," she said. She moved around behind me. "Now, I'd like you to stand with your back like this ..."

I felt one of her hands on the small of my back, and the other on my shoulder. She pushed and pulled to position me just so. She felt so *strong*. I tingled from the pressure and warmth in her touch, and the way she was standing so much closer to me than I expected.

"—touch your—"

She was whispering in my ear, and the feel of her breath on my skin made me dizzy. Was she still talking? What had she said?

"—hair."

I swallowed hard, and willed myself out of the homosexual mind spiral. "Sorry, what was that Haze?"

She giggled. It sounded angelic. "I said, I'd like you to put your hand up and touch your hair."

"Oh, okay! Uh, let me just—"

"I'll show you what I mean." She moved her hand off my shoulder, slid it down my arm, and took my hand. Her skin was soft, but her grip was firm and safe and guiding. She raised my hand up to the side of my face and placed my fingers against my hair.

I was starting to think I might lose consciousness.

"Very good," she said, "just like that. Hold that for me now, okay?"

"O ... kay ..." I said, with the minuscule amount of brain power I had left.

"Cool," she said. "I'm going to shoot a few frames and start finding some angles."

She let go of me and moved around to the other side of the roses. I heard myself whimper softly when her hands left me. I hoped against all hope that she didn't hear it.

"Okay," she said as she crouched down across from me, "here we go!"

With a practiced, fluid motion, she brought her camera to her eye, dialed in some settings, and fired the shutter. We were off and running.

Hazel and I made our way from one end of the rose garden to the other. She burned through so many rolls of film that I lost track. Though, admittedly, I was a bit distracted.

By the time we were a few rolls deep into the session, I was feeling something resembling actual confidence. My anxiety actually vanished for those few magical hours, and the world faded into background noise. There was only Hazel and me, connected by her camera.

I had, even if only briefly, reached a state of bliss. There in the rose garden, as I posed for Hazel, everything felt safe and right.

"Claire? You doing okay?" Hazel asked.

I snapped back to reality. She was staring at me with a bemused look on her face, and I realized I had completely spaced out.

"Oh, uh, yeah," I said. "Yeah! Sorry, I'm fine."

"Okay, cool. Just checking!" She grinned and nodded before putting the camera back up to her eye.

After we finished, we walked back together to the MAX station and hopped on a Blue Line train back downtown, where we'd make our transfers. This was where we parted ways, as I was going north to Hana's family's restaurant, and Hazel was heading back to her apartment in Ladd's Addition to the southeast.

Her train arrived first, and as it rolled into the station, we said our goodbyes for the evening.

"Okay, this is me," Hazel said. "I had so much fun today, for real."

"Me too," I said. "This was a really new thing for me, and I had a great time."

"Yeah?"

"Yeah!" I could feel the huge grin on my face. "You made me feel comfortable, and, like, special. Nobody's ever taken photos of me like that before."

She smiled and bit her lower lip. "I'm glad. I was hoping you'd feel special."

The way she said that made me blush all over again, but before I could form a response, the train had stopped and opened its doors.

"Alright, I gotta run," Hazel said. She reached down, took my hand, and gave it a squeeze. "Catch you later, rock star."

"Later, Haze."

Her hand lingered with mine for a long moment; then she let go, ran into the train, and took a seat. She gave me a little wave as the train pulled out of the station.

I would have stayed there, wandering through the fresh memories, but my train had already arrived. I dove through the doors right before they closed and found a place to sit.

Thankfully, the ride north and the walk to the restaurant would give me some quiet time to think.

※ ※ ※

Cass buried her face in her hands, muffling a scream. She looked up at me through her fingers.

"Claire. My dear. Have you even considered the possibility that this girl is into you?"

Hana had just brought out drinks and plates of food: spicy teriyaki tofu with rice, noodles with spinach and mushrooms, sautéed vegetables, sesame soy curls, and more. Everyone stared at me, as if they couldn't start eating until I answered.

"Who, Hazel?" I asked. "She's not into me. We're friends."

"*Claire,*" Cass said.

"Cass has a point," Hana said. "I half-expected you were going to say you confessed to her!"

"I knew there was something goin' on there," Nova said. "You gotta learn to trust my instincts, babe!"

I shook my head. "I mean, maybe, *maybe*, I have a little crush on her, but there's no way she reciprocates."

"What makes you say that?" Hana asked.

"Well, look at her! She's so cool. She dates cool girls."

"And as we all know," Cass said, "there's absolutely nothing cool about being a cute trans girl in a rock band made up entirely of queer magical girls."

"Hey, she only knows two-thirds of that," I protested.

Cass leaned across the table and stared into my eyes. "The point is, *you are cool.*" She leaned back, and I saw something flicker in her half-smile. "I know it can be hard to believe. I was worried about not being cool enough for every single one of my partners. I'm in a polycule with two girls and a guy, and I was sure none of them would go for me."

"But you're the coolest person here! Sorry, Nova."

"It's the truth!" Nova said through her straw.

"Call me cool if you want," Cass said, "but you are, too."

From her end of the table, Sara shook her head. "You're barely out, and you're already such a useless lesbian. I'm impressed."

I sighed. "Yeah. I'm feeling very seen right now."

"Well, I know the perfect way for you to heal," Hana giggled. "Eat up!"

Hana was right. Food was exactly what I needed. I sampled a little bit of everything, and it was all absurdly delicious. I eagerly went back for more, and as I ate a bite of one of the flavor explosions laid out before me, I looked over at her to express my joy.

"This food is incredible! I had no idea you were such a chef."

"Aw, thank you," Hana said, "though I'd hesitate to call myself a chef. I'm just following my parents' recipes!"

"Have your parents been in the restaurant business for a long time?"

She took a sip of beer. "Our family has a restaurant back in Osaka. It's been there since the Meiji Restoration, though we took it over from the original owner. My aunt and uncle still run it, which kind of set my parents free. We moved to Eugene when I was five, and they worked their way up to this place when we came here. I suppose if the whole 'magical girl rock band' thing doesn't work out, I could do this instead!"

"Yeah, about that," I said. "How did the 'magical-girl-slash-band' thing happen anyway?"

"I met Cass and Hana first," Sara said.

"That's right," Hana said. "When we were seventeen, we got involved Cass's community support group."

"Support group?" I asked.

"Mutual aid," Cass explained. "I help run it now, but back then, I was just a volunteer. We got our start helping out folks who'd been screwed over by ..." She paused to gesture vaguely with both hands. "... the *everything*. We work with groups that organize fundraisers to be the ones who do all the stuff they promise the money will do. We're the ones who give out the haircuts and haul the junk and cut the old folks' grass and set up their gardens every year."

"We got to be friends," Hana continued, "and we all shared music with each other. That's how we met Iris, at a vinyl record swap at a bar."

Sara smiled wistfully. "Right around the time the four of us decided to start a band, we had our awakenings. That basically sealed the deal. Then we met Nova a little while later."

Nova nodded. "Yup! Found me livin' in the woods out near Chiloquin with a stray cat, on account of family problems."

I paused, thinking she was telling a joke, but the punchline never came. "They found you living in the woods?"

She took a sip of her Shasta. "My dad didn't react too well to seein' what he thought was his thirteen-year-old son wearin' a dress. Got kicked out. If the gals hadn't found me, I dunno how I woulda ended up."

I watched her face and saw the muscles keeping her smile up stiffen, making little shadows creep into the corners of her mouth.

"No kid should have to deal with that," I said quietly.

"It's the past, babe," Nova said. "It's like they say, 'living well's the best revenge,' and I'm living real dang well now! Plus, I got a cute little kitty named Nebula out of it!" She pulled out her phone. After tapping through to the photos app, she turned it around to show me a selfie of her, sitting at her drum kit, with a beautiful white cat on her lap. "She's a lot bigger now than she was that night I found her in the woods!"

"Aww, that's adorable," I said. "And her name goes with yours."

Nova grinned. "Well, yeah! Space is cool!"

"Ah, family," Hana said, shaking her head. "You know, I still get passive-aggressive letters from my grandmother about my wicked homosexual ways."

"I know how that goes," I said. "I've got some people in my family like that, back in Texas."

"Yeah," Cass sighed. "Where would queer people be without family trauma?"

"Happy, well adjusted," Hana said.

"Flourishing, even," Sara added.

Nova shook her head. "If you ask me, I say family's a thing you pick, like how you pick the way you wanna be seen, y'know? It don't matter what your blood says. I got the me I wanted, and I got the family I wanted, right here!"

We all exchanged glances. Ever since I joined, I'd wondered if I'd ever feel fully comfortable around the group. They were all so cool, so experienced. I never actually expected to feel like I fit in.

"Yeah, I'll drink to that," Cass said, raising her pint glass. Sara raised hers as well.

"Yeah, same," I said, lifting mine.

"To being one big, happy, magical queer family," Hana said.

We reached across the table and clinked our glasses. After we'd all taken drinks of our respective beverages and gone back to eating, I noticed Sara chuckling quietly to herself.

"What is it?" I asked. "Something funny?"

"No, not funny," she said. "I just missed this. It's been a long time since we did one of these group dinners."

"Two years," Cass said.

Sara looked up and sighed. "Two years."

"I thought this was a regular thing," I said.

"It felt like a good time to bring it back," Hana said. "You deserve a real welcome, Claire."

I blushed and smiled back. Tonight, I felt like I belonged. "You're all very kind to me."

Nova grinned and gave a small, theatrical bow over her plate. "We ain't the guardians of song *and* heart for nothin', babe."

| 10 |

By the next day, the pain in my body from being thrown through a building just two nights before had disappeared entirely. I felt better than healed; I felt kind of fantastic, full of energy in a way I'd never felt before. And I knew exactly where to put that energy.

I walked to the Vault, enjoying the afternoon rain, a slow mist that seemed to calm the entire city. After checking in, I headed straight for the simulation room. I played through a full session, feeling a welcome burn in my muscles. It felt good to work my body again, put some practice between me and the memories of messing up in my debut fight.

As the day slid into the evening and I finished up, my wrist link buzzed with a call from Commander McCoy.

"*Agent Ryland, now that you're available, please report to the command center. We've got a job that needs doing.*"

"Of course, Commander," I said. "On my way."

The Portland Vault's command center was one of the rooms that most starkly showed how empty the place was these days. A large video screen dominated one wall, and I could easily see where the rows of computer consoles staffed by a team of support agents would have gone, with the commander's station at the head of the room looking out over everything.

These days, all those consoles were gone. A single computer desk sat alone in the middle of the otherwise empty room. Beside it, looking up at the video wall, were Commander McCoy, Saoirse, and Hana.

"Ah, Agent Ryland, good," the commander said.

"You said there was a job?" I asked.

Hana nodded. "There is! Though it's not a flashy one."

"But it's important," Saoirse added.

The commander tapped a few keys on the computer console and the wall display lit up with a map of Portland, covered in a giant green blob with a hole centered over downtown.

"The Starlight Alliance's Portland sensor network," she said. "Gives us complete coverage of the metro area."

"And before you ask," Saoirse piped in, "this isn't a spy network. We're not cops. I've had to give this speech over and over again, and frankly I—"

The commander's hand on her shoulder ended the rant.

Hana took up the slack. "The sensors just read the flow of magica and other kinds of unusual energy and maps everything out for us. You can think of it like a bunch of fancy weather stations!"

I looked back up at the screen. "That makes sense. What's the hole in the middle for?"

"The hole's the problem," the commander said, frowning. "We've lost contact with one of the sensors here in downtown, and somebody's gotta go fix it. Or, some*bodies*, which is where you and Agent Hasegawa come in."

I leaned close to Hana and whispered, "I don't know how to fix a magica sensor."

Hana smiled. "This is the perfect time to learn!"

"Used to be, we had people that'd go do this," Saoirse said, "but they all got reassigned."

"It sure was nice to have a staff," the commander grumbled. "I had to take this phone call myself! Hell of a way to run a railroad, if you ask me."

"Phone call?" I asked. "Who *calls* us about magica sensors?"

"Nobody calls the Starlight Alliance about magica sensors," Hana explained, "but they *do* call Willamette Electric & Infrastructure when a commercial 5G antenna with a slightly larger-than-normal box on the side starts acting up!"

"There's a lot of ways we hide in plain sight," the commander added.

Saoirse grabbed two piles of fabric from the computer console and held them up: a pair of commercial-grade worker's coveralls. "You two're going out there and getting my sensor back online. I'll monitor from here and guide you."

"Should be pretty straightforward," the commander said. "There's an IT engineer on-site who called it in. They'll be your contact. Give 'em some pleasantries, but don't let 'em look in the sensor box."

"Right, sure," I said. "Hey, where is this sensor, anyway?"

The commander smiled. "The roof of Big Pink."

I flinched. "The … *roof?*"

"C'mon, Claire," Hana grinned, "this is going to be fun! The view's amazing up there!"

Hana and I donned our baggy coveralls and made our way out through the Vault's access tunnels. We emerged from the hidden entrance beneath the Burnside Bridge and began our walk. The day's slow rain made every stretch of pavement shimmer and glow with reflected light.

Six blocks ahead of us, the forty-two-story skyscraper stood at the corner of Burnside and Fifth Avenue. It had a run-of-the-mill corporate name, but to everybody who lived here, the rectangular slab of granite and glass was simply called Big Pink. It was also the tallest building in the city. And we were going up to its roof.

I wasn't especially taken with this idea.

Hana, though, was as bright and bubbly as ever. Her dark brown ponytail swayed as she bounced along, a small tool bag slung over her shoulder.

"You seem surprisingly cheerful about going up that high," I said.

She smiled gently. "Aw, Claire, do you not like heights?"

"It's not that I don't like heights. It's more that I don't like what happens if I fall from them."

"Yeah, that's an understandable fear. Would it make you feel better to know that the sensor up there isn't near the edge? And there's a chest-height wall around the whole roof?"

"Well, maybe a little better, I guess. You've been up there before?"

"Oh yes, more than a few times now. With the Portland Vault's staff getting moved around to Seattle or California, we've had to take on a few new roles on top of magical girl."

I glanced over at her. "Is this staff thing because of what happened to Iris?"

"In large part, yes," she said, her voice growing more quiet. "It rattled us. Hurt the band's popularity. You might not think that's a big deal, but the Alliance has its own politics. Seattle's become the big magical girl city up here, so the resources get moved around."

"Which just makes our jobs harder," I pointed out.

As she always seemed to, Hana chose optimism. "You're not wrong, but it's let me branch out a little. Not only have I done this before, I'm also arc welder certified!"

"Wow," I said, sincerely. "Bass player, arc welder, magical girl—you're a real Renaissance woman."

She laughed. "I just like learning things, and—ooh, Claire! Let's stop up here for a second!"

We were about to cross Second Avenue to Ankeny Alley, and ahead of us I saw multiple bars and the glowing pink sign of Marie's XXX Donuts. "You, uh, need a beer? Or a cruller?"

"No, silly. C'mon, I'm not a tourist! There's a little juice cart around the corner. I'll show you!"

We dashed across the street and down the alley. There were quite a few people out and about, but if any of them recognized us from the band, they didn't indicate it. It seemed our electrician getups were at least reasonably convincing.

At the end of the alley, where it exited onto Third, we veered left, away from the donut shop. There, open to a small makeshift plaza of potted bushes, tables, and chairs, stood a small white food cart. Above the ordering window, a hand-painted cartoon medieval woman in a bustier beckoned passersby with handfuls of fruits and vegetables, next to a logo reading JUICE WENCH in block lettering. When we reached the window, a woman who was the spitting image of the titular Juice Wench on the sign leaned out of the window and gave us a broad grin.

"Well, what can I do for ye this fine eve, my queens?" she asked.

"I'll have what she's having," I said.

"Two orange-pineapple juices to go, please, Delilah," Hana said.

"Oh! Hana! Didn't recognize you in that getup," Delilah the Juice Wench said. "Coming right up! Who's your cute friend?"

I felt myself blushing. "Um ... I, uh ... Claire."

"She just joined the band," Hana said. "She's our new keyboard player!"

Delilah the Juice Wench flipped switches on an array of industrial-strength juicing machines while she talked. "Right on! Well, any friend of Hana's a friend of mine." In a flash, she poured and slid two cups of orange-pineapple juice across the window sill of her cart.

"Lightning fast, as always," Hana said as she held her phone up to the cart's payment kiosk.

"Always the finest service in this 'ere tavern," Delilah the Juice Wench said. "Have a good night out in the realm, my queens!"

I looked over at Hana as we resumed our walk to Big Pink. "You're popular."

She smiled and shrugged. "I used to be shy when I was younger. Portland's been good to me! This city's changed a lot, but I still love it."

"I can relate to Portland being beneficial."

"I'd say so," she giggled. "Hopefully, that means you're having a good time with all this."

"Being a girl, or being a magical girl, or being in the band?"

"All three!"

There was never any doubt in my mind that being a girl was something I needed, and I loved it now that I had it. Being a *magical* girl, of course, had been a very unexpected surprise—as had being recruited for my favorite band—but for all the challenges I'd gone through, I felt genuinely happy being in Magica Riot.

"It's been amazing," I said. "I've had anxiety about all of it, but I have anxiety a lot of the time about all kinds of things, so that's not new."

"Sounds like you've dealt with it for a long time."

"Yeah. I always worried that I couldn't be a girl because I wouldn't be cute enough. Stopped playing in bands after high school because I thought I'd never able to do it for real. Being a magical girl has helped me feel a lot more confident about everything. Well, I mean, as long as I don't have to sing."

"You don't think you'll ever want to sing?" Hana asked gently.

"It's not like I hate the idea," I said. "Just don't love my voice. Nervous that it sounds too much like ... well, y'know ... the old me."

"I think your voice is lovely, but I completely understand being nervous. We've got plenty of time for more gigs. There's no rush. It might have seemed like it, since you joined in such an abrupt way."

I laughed. "It was a shock, yeah, but now I know that's just how Nova operates."

"Yeah, that's Nova for you! Always ready to push the rules." She sighed. "Sometimes, that energy gets her into trouble."

I glanced over at her. Something had been on my mind about Nova, and this might be my best chance to ask about it.

"Hey, speaking of Nova, what's the deal with the 'watch the language' thing?"

Hana shook her head. "Heroes don't curse."

"They don't?"

"That's Nova's thing. Her parents cursed up a storm when they got mad at her. So we don't."

I felt a lump in my throat; I should have put the pieces together sooner. "Oh god ... uh, gosh, I mean. I had no idea."

"Gosh will do nicely," she smiled. "I think she's on your case about it because Iris cursed, too. I don't know, maybe she wants you to—" She stopped and faced me, giving me an apologetic look. "Sorry, I know this is kind of a heavy subject. The thing is, it's like we said at dinner. We're a family, but we're a bit of a mixed-up, complicated little family, and we just try our best to make it work. I probably should have said something before, but we haven't had to bring anybody in from the outside until now, so we're making this up as we go."

"It's okay, I get it," I said. I felt tears welling in my eyes. "And I want to say, I'm really proud to be a part of that mixed-up, complicated family."

Hana beamed at me. "You have no idea how happy that makes me!" She dove at me, and before I could process it, she had me in a hug.

I wrapped my arms around her and hugged back, getting my tears out before we moved on with our job.

We reached Big Pink as the evening sunset began to fade. After giving our names and cover story to the security guard, he gave us an access card and directed us to a spot halfway up on the twenty-first floor, where we'd meet the IT engineer who'd put in the call.

One elevator ride later, we stood in front of a nondescript door labeled "SERVER CLOSET." Beyond it, I heard the constant whoosh of dozens of computer fans.

Hana knocked on the door and called out to whoever was inside. "Hello! Willamette Electric and Infrastructure here! We've come to look at that 5G repeater!"

Several long moments passed before the door slowly swung open, the noise of the hardware inside instantly jumping up in volume.

Stepping into the server closet was like stepping into a jungle; fans blew air in all directions, hot swirling with cold, wires exploding like vines from the computers mounted in racks from floor to ceiling along the walls. At the far end of the glorified hallway was what appeared to be a tiny child curled up, but as the figure stood I realized it belonged to an adult, at least Nova's age. Asymmetrical black clothing hung like drapery, concealing any indication of form. A shaggy angled bob of cyan hair obscured one eye, the other gleaming in the blinking green lights behind chunky black-framed glasses.

"Hey," they said. "You're not like here to rob the building or steal some kind of important document from an office or whatever are you?" They spoke in a flat, mumbling monotone, without intonation or even pauses for breaths.

"No, nothing like that," Hana said. "We're here to take a look at that antenna up on the roof?"

"You called that in, right?" I asked.

They nodded, almost imperceptibly. "Oh yeah that was me totally sorry about that you just kind of get up in your own head when you're here after hours and you have to make up your own fun anyway yeah that was me I'm Hikari resident late-night IT contractor."

Hana smiled. "I'm Hana, and this is Claire."

"I like your outfit," I said.

"Oh wow thanks," Hikari said. "It's the attire of my people you know those of us who live in the shadows of the virtual aether or whatever and it doesn't give away too much about my non-specific biological construct you know gotta keep people guessing."

"What happened with the antenna?" Hana asked.

"The thing overloaded and tripped a breaker that took down a few of my network switches here," Hikari said, gesturing to the rack units they'd been examining, "so I had to do a little creative rewiring to keep the building's Ethernet up and running I don't know what's so important here but all these corporate types start yelling if they can't download their spreadsheets so it is what it is."

"That shouldn't take us too long to fix," Hana said. "We'll head up and take a look. Once we're done, we'll check in with you so you can test everything on your end. Sound good?"

"Yeah for sure," Hikari said. "I'll be here I don't really have anywhere else to be hey by the way you look familiar have I see you somewhere?"

I froze as my brain immediately leapt to the worst-case scenario. "Nope! Probably not! We're just electricians! Normal electricians!" Out of the corner of my eye, I saw Hana smile and shake her head at my awkwardness.

If Hikari thought my response was strange, they didn't say so. "Huh well okay maybe I'm mistaken then yeah just let me know when you're done good luck up there my new bejumpsuited friends."

Hana and I took an elevator to the tower's top floor, then climbed a flight of stairs up to the rooftop door.

"Are you feeling okay, Claire?" Hana asked. "If you're not up for this, it's really okay."

I took a deep breath. "No, no. I'm good. Let's just get it done. As long as I don't look over the edge, I'll be okay."

Hana smiled, then pushed the rooftop door open.

The tower's roof was dominated by a helipad in the center. Around the outside, pieces of equipment and antennas jutted up in random places, the tallest of which was a mast of crisscrossed metal beams.

"That's where the sensor is," Hana said. "Let's go. It'll be fixed before you know it!"

I kept my focus away from the roof's edges as we walked over to the mast. Several different antennas and radio dishes were mounted to it at different heights; to my great relief, the one Hana pointed to as the sensor was near the bottom. It looked like a fairly normal antenna, and I would not have been able to identify it as anything unusual from the outside.

"We need to fix it, and we'll need to recalibrate it," Hana said. "The new Grand Sovereign hotel tower down at Tenth and Alder is tall enough to throw off the downtown grid."

I glanced off to the south. That new hotel—still under construction—was easy to spot. Its concrete frame stretched up into the sky, rivaling Big Pink's height, and glistening glass panels climbed about halfway up, marking off construction progress. Work had stopped on it recently, though, due to a construction worker's strike over pay and safety conditions.

"Oh yeah," I said. "That thing. It's awfully big."

"Yeah. It's an eyesore, if you ask me," Hana said. "A playground for one-percenters who'll come to town and sip wine at thousands of dollars per bottle while they complain about people sleeping on the street."

I was surprised to hear the pointed anger beneath her words. "You're not wrong. I didn't know you got so fired up about that kind of thing."

She nodded. "That's the kind of change in Portland I don't like. That's why Sara and I got involved in Cass's community support group."

"That makes sense," I said. I looked down at the antenna itself; it ended in a large metal box with a hinged door. "Could regular people even get through that?"

"Nope, not a chance," Hana said. "This lock is keyed to magica. You either have to be a magica user yourself or have specifically attuned thaumatite to open it. I'll show you!"

She laid her hand against the lock, and with a brief flash of green energy, the lock clicked open. She swung the door open, revealing a complicated assortment of circuit boards, wires, and thaumatite crystals inside the device.

"First, we need to figure out what's caused this one to misbehave," she said. "We'll just try to energize the crystals and we—"

"You denied it but I know your secret now," a distinctive monotone mumble interrupted from behind us. We turned to find Hikari standing there, as expressionless as before, holding a battered old laptop covered in stickers ranging from pride flags to Linux memes.

Panic rushed through me; had we been found out so easily? I started running through the conversation, trying to find anything we'd said that would have given away our magical girl secret.

"Claire," Hana whispered, "why don't you go chat with our new friend, so they can't see what I'm doing."

I nodded and stood up. "Uh, hey, Hikari! What are you talking about?"

"You were very sneaky about it but you can't fool me I know exactly what you are," Hikari said.

I walked over and positioned myself directly in Hikari's line of sight, too nervous to attempt anything more subtle. "Listen, whatever it is you think you know, I can explain."

"You don't need to explain anything I know you're in Magica Riot," Hikari said.

I stopped cold. Hikari knew we were magical girls. Our one big rule had been broken. How did they figure it out? How were we going to get out of this?!

"Hikari..."

"I didn't recognize you because of the coveralls but now it's obvious I've seen you play before I was even at the Cosmic Club show."

Fear crashed into relief. "Oh! Oh yeah! We're a band! Yeah, you got us, alright."

It was almost impossible to tell, but I swore I saw Hikari crack the tiniest smile. "That's awesome you all rock in ways both general and specific right like there's big gender feels on those albums which I appreciate especially when delivered in a face-melting sense."

I smiled back. "I know what you mean, yeah. That's part of why I loved the band, before I joined."

"Oh that's right yeah you're new," Hikari said. "The show got cut off but I liked what you did in that verse and chorus I heard."

"Thanks. Yeah, the power outage was rough."

"I guess that explains why you all ran off though right you left because you're all secretly electricians and duty called."

"Well, uh—"

Hikari kept going. "Hey no I get it totally it sucks how artists have to get jobs to survive out there it's brutal until we're saved by fully automated luxury gay space communism I actually do some DJ-ing and make electronic music in my bedroom I do house shows sometimes I should give you my card well it's more of a sticker anyway don't worry I'm on your side solidarity forever fight the man till you're in the ground that's what I say."

I marveled at their lung capacity. "Yeah, it definitely sucks. I appreciate it, one musician to another."

"For sure for sure," Hikari said. "Hey how much does the electrician thing pay anyway because I'm not exactly drowning in loyalty here I don't even get windows in that server closet and they frown on me taking breaks in the tenants' offices like come on sorry I don't fit into your business casual Fridays there Deborah but a construct's gotta have a little water fountain action sometimes hey what's going on back there why's that antenna glowing?"

I glanced back at Hana, who was still working in the magical depths of the sensor's hardware. The telltale glow of magica was clearly visible.

"Uh, well," I stammered in nervous desperation, "it's ... RGB lights."

"Gamer aesthetics on a 5G antenna huh," Hikari said. "Okay that's a little gauche but I'm not one to judge you should see my apartment I can't really throw too many stones from my glass house of modded Dreamcasts."

Gotta keep them talking. "Do you play a lot of games?" I asked. I began a shuffling rotation around Hikari, bringing them along in my orbit as we traded places. Hikari thankfully kept their eyes on me, and eventually, their back was toward Hana.

"Claire I don't know how to answer that question in a way that won't make you think less of me but I guess I have some skills you might even call them mad hey do you play Dark Souls?"

"Dark Souls? Oh, uh, no, I'm terrible at those," I said, searching my brain for video games I enjoyed. "I'm more New Vegas trans than Soulsborne trans."

"Oh yeah New Vegas totally I get you I don't know anything about it other than the basics but yeah much respect you gotta have your thing that keeps your brain happy in this ever-changing world in which we live in."

"For sure, yeah." In the background, I saw Hana throw her arms up in frustration; I'd need to bring out my big guns.

Godspeed, I thought, *to both of us.*

"Soooo, Hikari," I said, "what's your third favorite thing about Dark Souls?"

Hikari took a deep breath and began. "Well that's a big question you know there's a lot of different facets of FromSoft's design ethos that really appeal to me I guess chief among which is the way the games teach you to get better at them through careful practice of skill and..."

Over their shoulder, I kept an eye on Hana. The glow inside the sensor was sputtering and flickering now as she became visibly annoyed with it.

All the while, Hikari kept going.

"... and of course the world design which rewards careful exploration and learning the environment so that..."

Hana was now *kicking* the sensor.

"... the way lore is delivered in such a subtle way that really makes you pay attention to details that..."

With one last kick, the sensor sprung to life. The crystals glowed vibrantly as a blast of energy shot out and blew Hana back a couple of feet.

Hikari looked up into the sky. "... poison swamps though woah hey are there fireworks tonight or something?"

"Oh, uh, m-maybe," I said. My eyes went wide as I watched Hana scramble back to the sensor and slam the door shut again, blocking off the glow just as Hikari turned back to her.

"Yeah, that's it! I think somebody set off fireworks across the river!" Hana shouted.

"Makes sense yeah you're gonna get that," Hikari said.

"Um, so, is the antenna okay?" I asked.

"I think so," Hana said. "Hikari, could you run whatever tests you need to run? Claire and I will need to head out soon so we can file our report and get paid."

"For sure for sure gotta make that bank I hear you," Hikari said. They flipped open their laptop and set it down on the roof; several seconds of furious typing later, they seemed pleased. "Yeah looks like it's not interfering anymore all's well that ends well as they say thanks for getting out here so quick."

Hana stood. "It's not a problem at all! We've got to run now, though. It was nice to meet you, Hikari!"

"Yeah," I said, "have a good rest of your night."

"I will try to have the best time I can in my windowless nerd bunker," Hikari said. "Nice meeting you also your band is rad please here take these maybe we can trade tracks sometime."

They handed us two shimmery foil stickers with a minimalist line-art drawing of an utterly neutral face, presumably a self-portrait, and a single web address underneath that read HIKARI DOT PIZZA.

Hana flashed them a star-bright smile. "This is great! I know just where I'll put this."

"We'll check out your stuff when we, uh, get off the clock," I said.

Hikari nodded. "Cool cool alright keep it chill and sleazy my friends."

***

Back down on the street, Hana seemed preoccupied. She frowned and shook her head, as if trying to tackle a problem.

"Uh, something wrong?" I asked.

"Claire, somebody tampered with the sensor. I found wires disconnected from the thaumatite receiver."

"Who would mess with one of our sensors?"

"The question is, who *could*. Regular people can't get through those locks. Somebody's either got thaumatite, or the ability to wield magica."

I felt a chill run down my back. "It's the mystery girls."

"We don't know for sure, but they have to be a strong contender." She sighed. "Let's get back to the Vault and report in. Saoirse can run a diagnostic to make sure everything's okay. This is giving me a bad feeling."

PART TWO

Blooms

| 11 |

The next few days were relatively calm, apart from a couple of small Pandora Corruption fights. Saoirse checked out the sensor network and—despite the evidence that somebody had accessed the sensor—she didn't find any oddities in the system. Because the mystery girls hadn't reappeared, and we didn't have much else to go on, we had to wait and see.

With no gigs in the immediate future, I was able to relax a little bit, spend time with the band and Hazel, and focus on my training. Which was how I found myself on Thursday afternoon in magical girl mode in the simulation room with Sara and Nova, running combat drills while Dr. Barrera monitored our vital signs.

"Disorient, assault! Close distance and engage!" Sara shouted.

For the fourth time that morning, we faced a quintet of Pandora creatures. Nova hung out behind us, slamming out a disorienting rhythm on her drums, while Sara and I raced toward the fight.

I ran beside her, firing bolts of magica at the holographic creatures while she played chunky, overdriven chords to charge up her guitar. We'd been training with this particular program for a week now, so I knew my next moves practically by heart.

We reached the creatures, and as Sara swung her guitar at one of their heads, I pushed off with my leg and rolled to the left between two others. I fired a shot at one and bashed into the other with the body of my keytar, then sprung back up to my feet. My muscles strained as I reversed direction and prepared to hurl myself at the creatures' backs to jab them and bring them down.

I was running on highly practiced routine—right up to the moment when one of the creatures did something that wasn't in the last dozen runs. It spun around and slammed its arm into my stomach, driving me into the floor of the simulation room. Before I could react, it was on top of me, piercing its arm spike down into my sternum.

This final impact never came. Before the creature drove its arm into my chest, the simulator's safety protocols engaged and the spike dissolved into digital mist.

"Pause program and end immersion mode," Sara said.

The four creatures froze in mid-movement and the room lights came back on to full brightness.

I flopped back against the cool metallic floor. "Okay, what happened there?"

Sara, Nova, and Dr. Barrera walked over and looked down at me.

"You did great," Sara said as she offered me her hand. "The computer just figured you out."

Dr. Barrera extended her hand as well. "How are you feeling, Claire?"

I took their hands and got back on my feet. "The only thing hurt is my pride, I guess. What do you mean, the computer figured me out?"

"Once ya get good enough, the computer starts to throw curve balls at ya," Nova said.

Sara nodded. "It's scoring you every time, and learning how you fight. As you improve, it mixes up the creatures' patterns and tries to catch you by surprise."

I looked back at the paused creatures. "Getting laid out after doing it fine a dozen times doesn't feel great, though."

"Don't look at it like that. It means you're good enough now that the system's encouraging you to improvise."

"I'm ... good enough?"

"Yeah. It's moved you up from 'beginner' to 'intermediate.' Instead of just copying basic attacks, it's letting you start thinking for yourself. That's the next skill you'll focus on."

"That's kind of intimidating," I said. I took a deep breath and exhaled as I thought about the implications. "What if the stuff I come up with messes things up? Or I get in your way?"

"Claire, we're a team," Sara said. "We cover each other."

"Exactly, babe," Nova said. "The more ya do it, the more we'll know how ya think!"

Sara smiled broadly and gave my shoulder a squeeze. "What I'm trying to get across here is that we trust you to find your own personal fighting style now. The keytar's a flexible instrument. You've been using it mostly to deal damage, but you can cross over into support roles, too. I want you to be yourself out there and grow into something that works for you."

"I appreciate the confidence," I said, smiling back.

Sara's wrist link chimed with a call and she raised it to answer. "This is Ward."

"Agent Ward, I've got a sensor report I'd like to go over with you," the commander said. *"Could you come to my office?"*

"Sure. We were just wrapping up here. On my way." She nodded to Nova and me and the doctor before she left. "You're doing great, Claire. Just make sure to keep your eyes open and adapt."

"I will, for sure."

As Sara walked out of the room and the door closed behind her, I noticed Nova and Dr. Barrera exchanging curious looks.

"I'm so happy to see this," Dr. Barrera said.

"For real! It's like the old days," Nova agreed.

"What's that?" I asked.

Nova grinned at me. "Boss lady! That right there? That's the old Sara! That's the one I remember from back in the day. Y'know... before."

Dr. Barrera sighed and smiled happily. "I haven't seen that side of her for two years. She was always a very warm and gentle person. She just doesn't show it directly these days."

Nova put her arm around me and squeezed. "You got here just when we needed ya, Claire babe."

I stared at the closed door where Sara had exited and thought about my time with her. I didn't have the context of knowing her before, but I *had* noticed that she seemed more cheerful.

I'd never considered that my arrival had anything to do with it.

After training, Saoirse asked me to bring my keytar to the armory. She wanted to use the data from training to calibrate something on the instrument, so I made my way down there while Dr. Barrera took Nova back to the med bay for a check-up.

When I walked into the armory, Cass and Hana were also there, hanging out around the secure instrument lockboxes while Saoirse toiled away at her workbench.

"What are you two doing in here?" I asked.

"Saoirse is putting new frets on my bass and recalibrating the focused magica emitters on Cass's guitar," Hana said.

"So we were talking music," Cass said. "Swapping some favs."

Hana nodded. "She and I have highly influenced each other's playlists over the years."

"Nice," I said. "I'm here for the recalibration, too."

"Yeah you are," Saoirse called out from her workbench. "Go on and leave the keytar here so I can get you sorted."

I focused and pulled the keytar over from the aetheric plane and laid it on Saoirse's workbench. "It's in your capable hands."

"Flatterer," Saoirse said as she smirked at me. I'd gotten to know her moods well enough that I could just about see the twinkle in her eye through her goggles. She picked up Hana's bass, held it aloft, and waved across the room. "Here you go, Miss Hana. Should be ready to go."

"Thank you so much," Hana said. She recalled her bass to her, and slapped and plucked out a few quick riffs. "Oh yes, this is wonderful! The buzz I was getting on the D-string is gone. Excellent work!"

"It's my pleasure. Now, Miss Cass, Miss Claire, it's your turn. I can run the calibration on both your instruments together. Just give me a few minutes."

"That's cool," Cass said.

"Yeah, sounds good," I said. I walked over in Cass and Hana's direction while Saoirse went to work on our instruments.

The armory, like every other part of the Portland Vault, looked like it had once been packed full of much more equipment than it was now. Apart from Saoirse's workbench and tools, the only other features in the room these days were the lockboxes that lined one wall, and assorted piles of parts.

One of the piles held something that looked distinctly like a robotic arm, which seemed odd.

"Hey, uh, what's that for?" I asked Cass and Hana as I nodded toward the arm.

"Saoirse's robot girlfriend," Cass said with a grin.

"I *heard* that," Saoirse said. "Like all good armorers, I have some side projects. This job gives me access to great hardware. That one's an idea for a prototype android support unit, thank you very much. The fact that it will happen to look like a girl is ... unrelated."

Cass and Hana looked at me and shrugged, so I decided to drop the subject and move on. My eyes were drawn next to the lockbox instrument cases on the wall; most were empty, but several at one end held instruments.

"How about those?" I asked. "What are all those instruments up there?"

"Decommissioned," Saoirse said, without looking up from her bench.

"Those belonged to girls who are no longer active," Hana said.

"No longer active," I repeated, as I took another look at the instruments. It was at that moment that I noticed one at the end of the row was another, very familiar keytar, one I'd seen in old band photos.

Iris's keytar.

The word "decommissioned" took on a much more chilling connotation in my mind. I had known, of course, that magical girls could die. That was part of the reason I was even here. Seeing her keytar here now, along with several other instruments whose owners would never be coming back for them, made the danger of this life hit hard.

"I guess I never thought about how many sad stories there had to be," I said.

Cass and Hana exchanged looks, then glanced up at the lockboxes.

"Oh, Claire, no," Cass said. "It's not like that."

"What do you mean? That's Iris's keytar, isn't it? So those must be from other girls who passed."

"A couple, sure," Hana said, "but most of them belong to the retirees."

"The retirees?"

"Being a magical girl is dangerous, absolutely," Hana continued, "but it's not just death left and right. Sometimes, girls just finish their careers and need to take a break."

"And some have to, when they get messed up by the wall," Cass added.

That term was foreign to me. "What's the wall?"

"When you hit the limit of your power, but you feel like there's something else beyond that limit," Hana said.

"Wait, there's a name for it?" I asked. That sounded exactly like the brief sensation I'd had during the fight near Cosmic Club.

"So you've felt it," Cass said.

"I did, yeah."

Cass shook her head. "Nobody knows what's up with it. It's kind of intoxicating, and some girls, they get obsessed with finding a way to break through. So they lose their grip, and eventually, they gotta retire."

"The important thing is to manage that feeling," Hana said. "Don't lose yourself in it. As long as you keep that in mind, you can have a long career as a magical girl!"

"Exactly, yeah," Cass said. "The Alliance loses more girls to that than to fatalities."

"Death just is a possibility, not a foregone conclusion," Hana added.

I was about to reply when our wrist links chirped with an incoming notification from the commander.

"Agent Coates, Agent Hasegawa, Agent Ryland, Agent Nova, please report to the command center."

Saoirse looked up and waved us off. "I'll have your instruments ready in ten. Go see what the boss wants."

Cass hit the reply button on her link. "We're on our way, Commander. Heading down from the armory now."

* * *

The command center was relatively busy when we arrived. Sara and Nova stood next to Dr. Barrera and the commander, gazing up at the big screen as it displayed a map of Earth with several glowing dots of various colors in different cities.

"Busy day?" Cass asked.

The commander gestured at the screen. "Not bad, really. Tokyo HQ sent Storm Maiden after that corporate creep who was trying to build a robot army. Took him down pretty decisively."

"They totally kicked butt," Nova said.

"That was the big news item," the commander continued, "until the good doc walked in. Now that y'all are all here, we can get started. She's got some news for us."

"Good news, I hope," Hana said.

Dr. Barrera sighed. "I wish it was so simple. The matter at hand concerns the mystery girls and those energy readings that accompanied them."

The video wall switched to a map of the city's Central Eastside, with overlaid sensor readings from the night of the show. The Pandora Corruption monsters were labeled as such, while the other readings appeared as a fuzzy blur labeled "PDX-204-X."

Dr. Barrera continued. "The two-hundred-and-fourth unknown reading collected in Portland to date. Now, you girls ran into three distinct beings, correct?"

"That's right, yeah," Cass said.

Three humanoid silhouettes joined the map, labeled PDX-204-X-1, -2, and -3.

"It's been difficult to fully analyze," Dr. Barrera continued, "due to the imprecise nature of the citywide sensor grid. However, two of you—Cass and Claire—got closer readings."

"A little too close," I said, "and then very far away."

"Right. Your encounter provided us with much clearer data via your wrist links."

The blurry blobs sharpened into distinct shapes on the screen, and complicated overlapping waveforms appeared beside the first and third silhouettes.

"I've never seen energy like that before," Sara said.

"What are we looking at, doctor?" the commander asked.

"I'd never seen this, either," Dr. Barrera said, "until I realized this isn't one energy signature, but *two*. Two distinct energies, intermingled, carrying and reenforcing each other."

On the screen, the waveform split apart.

"If that's the case," Hana said, "are you able to identify them separately?"

Dr. Barrera frowned slightly. "That's the problem. The first signature is *almost* the Pandora Corruption signature."

"Almost?" Cass asked.

"It's eighty percent the same. The other twenty percent isn't even close to a match for anything in the database."

"Okay, that ain't great, but what about the second one?" Nova asked.

Dr. Barrera tapped her link. "That signature is nothing, until you invert it."

The second waveform folded in and out on itself, and suddenly lit up in green with a text box beside it. I felt the room grow quieter as we all realized what we were seeing.

SIGNATURE: MAIDEN ENERGY. CLASSIFICATION: MAGICAL GIRL. MATCH: 100%.

Hana let out a long, low whistle. "So Cass and Claire *did* see magical girls."

"In a sense, yes," Dr. Barrera said, "though I don't think we've got conventional magical girls here. There's some connection between those girls and the Pandora Corruption, and I'm not sure what it is."

"Well, this complicates things," Sara said.

The commander frowned at the screen, then took a deep breath and exhaled. "You're right about that. If those are magical girls, then they're people, and we ain't exactly in the business of executions. So, we gotta figure out what they're up to. See if we can talk with them. Next time they show up, I want you girls to—"

The blaring of the Vault's warning system interrupted her. The screen switched to a map of the north side of the city with sensor blips in the St. Johns neighborhood, and bold red text appeared at the top of the screen.

PANDORA CORRUPTION INCURSION DETECTED.

Another set of blips appeared a short distance from the Pandora readings, labeled PDX-204-X-1, PDX-204-X-2, and PDX-204-X-3.

"Speak of the devil," Cass said.

The commander turned to face us. "Looks like you girls are off to St. Johns. Get out there and see if you can figure out what the mystery girls are up to. The sun's still up, but hopefully, there won't be any witnesses around."

I tapped my wrist link and called the armory. "Hey, Saoirse, are our instruments ready? We've got to head out."

"I was just about to give you a ring," she responded. *"Go ahead and call them. They're ready to go."*

"Thanks." I focused on my keytar and felt it slip through the aether and materialize around me, just as Cass's guitar did the same. After giving them a quick check, we sent them back into the aetheric plane to wait for us.

"Alright," Sara said, "let's get to Vancent and hit the road. We've got a date we can't miss."

| 12 |

With Sara at the wheel, Vancent Price blasted up Highway 30 and across the St. Johns Bridge, and parked in the industrial area near the neighborhood's main street. After a quick check on the sensor readings, we got out and followed them via our wrist links, heading toward the next block.

The sensors had indicated the Pandora Corruption creatures and the mystery girls were very close to each other. As we rounded the corner onto the street where the readings were strongest, we weren't prepared for just *how* close.

"You all seeing what I'm seeing?" Cass asked.

Farther down the street, in the fading late afternoon sun, stood three Pandora creatures. Beside them were the trio of mystery girls. We could get a decent look at them for the first time: the violet-haired girl and the blonde, plus the third, who had a midnight blue bob. Just as before, they were dressed in short black corset dresses and boots. All of them had the same metallic masks around their glowing red eyes.

And each had plunged tube-like devices encrusted with thaumatite crystals into the shells of the creatures. The devices slurped out the black goop inside while the creatures stood transfixed.

"What are they doing?" Hana asked.

"It's almost like they're taking samples," I said.

"Whatever they're doing, I'm done watching," Sara said. She stepped forward and cupped her hands around her mouth. "Hey! Hold it right there!"

Violet girl smiled and turned toward us, speaking in an affected lower register. "Oh my! I was wondering when you girls might show up."

"And just who do you think we are?"

Violet girl laughed. "Oh, please. You don't think I'd recognize *the* Magica Riot? I know all about you! We've had our eyes on you for some time. Tell me, did you enjoy the power outage while you played your little show?"

"That was you," Hana said. "Of course. I guess you were the ones messing with our sensors, too."

"Guilty as charged," violet girl said. "You're too fun to play with. Honestly, you're lucky this is Portland. You girls aren't exactly subtle! Anywhere else, you'd stand out like sore thumbs! But *we* see you."

Cass glared at her. "Then how about you tell us who you are."

"Oh, I dunno," the blonde said. "Might be more fun if you don't know!"

Blue hair nodded. "The mystery girls who beat you down with a single punch."

"Actually, I'm feeling generous," violet girl said. "Maybe I'll let you have this one. Keep things a little fair, since you're so utterly outmatched otherwise, going up against the superior intellect and breathtaking beauty that you see before—"

"Just get on with it," Sara interrupted.

Violet girl pouted and rolled her eyes. "Ugh, *fine*. You're no fun. You find yourselves in the presence of…"

"Menagerie Burst," blue girl said.

Blonde stepped forward. "Menagerie Blaze."

"And I am the illustrious, the radiant, Menagerie Bloom," violet girl said. "We are the Menagerie, as would hopefully be obvious."

"How appropriate," Hana said.

"What are you doing to those Pandora Corruption creatures?" Sara asked.

Bloom sighed and shook her head. "Such ignorant, inadequate terminology. It showcases how limited your point of view is. 'The Pandora Corruption.' A crude dismissal of finely honed tools of chaos."

"Mistress was right about you five," Burst said. "Truly sad."

"No appreciation for the divine handiwork of those so far beyond your own understanding," Bloom added.

Nova frowned at them. "Mistress? Understanding? The flam are you talking about?"

"New girl," Bloom said, looking directly at me, "do you see the kind of mental purgatory you've been roped into? You'll never truly understand the nature of existence if you spend your time with these girls. Enlightenment will escape you—until we bring it to you, of course."

"Oh no, leave me out of this," I said, "and answer the question. What are you talking about?"

Bloom's red eyes stared into me. "These physical forms were like you, once. Mistress created us to wield them for a higher purpose. *Her* purpose, which is all that matters. To show the world the value of submission and service to her beautiful plans." She gestured at the Pandora creatures. "Soon, they'll understand again, and they'll rejoin her cosmic army. Then, at last, we will bring enlightenment to the rest of you. The world will finally be unified under her heart, as it nearly was before."

"I don't think so," Cass said. "You're gonna be real disappointed."

"We're not going to let anything like that happen," Sara said. "Hand over those devices, or we'll take them from you."

Bloom withdrew her device from the nearest creature. "These? No, I don't think we will. The data they gather is far too important. We're so very close to unlocking the knowledge we need."

Blaze and Burst pulled their own devices out, and the three Pandora creatures dissolved, just as they did when we killed them.

"Sadly, these three specimens of Mistress's legacy had to be sacrificed," Bloom continued, "but their loss serves a greater good." She latched the device to an attachment on her belt, and turned back to us. "Which now leaves us with the far more interesting question of what to do about you."

"Starting to look like things are gonna have to get unpleasant, boss," Cass said.

"Agreed," Sara said. "I've had enough of this. Ladies, let's go to work!"

With a flash of magica, our microphones appeared, and we brought them to our lips.

"Maidensong harmony power ... go live!"

The towering swirls of rainbow energy blasted up around us and lifted us from the ground as our street clothes vanished. With power coursing through us, we pirouetted in mid-air as our costumes materialized on our bodies.

When we emerged from our transformations, Sara glared at the Menagerie and stood her ground. "We are the guardians of song and heart! Servants of the darkness, be silenced by the song of Magica Riot!"

Bloom ran a hand through her hair and sighed. "That really does take a while."

Cass called forth her guitar. "Yeah, but *this* is much faster." She let loose a bolt of magical energy at Bloom, who sidestepped it and grinned back.

"Finally! Some proper action," Bloom laughed.

The Menagerie girls ran straight for us. We conjured our instruments and split up as Sara began to play the opening chords of "Charlatan," a song from the band's fourth album.

"C'mon, babes!" Nova shouted. "Let's knock these girls out!"

She let loose with a drum fill. Percussive shockwaves surrounded Bloom and Blaze and pummeled them from all sides.

Cass continued sniping them while Sara charged, swinging her guitar in sync with Nova's beats as she sang. *"You're a charlatan with everything to lose! Your world comes crashing down with a single wrong move!"*

In the corner of my eye, I saw Burst break off and run for Nova. I nodded at Hana, who used her bass to throw up a wall of magica in her path.

I waited for the inevitable crash, but the impact never came.

Burst leapt skyward over Hana's wall, before a spinning disk of fiery red magica appeared in the air above her. She flipped around and hit the disk with her feet, and with a flash of light, she shouted and launched off it directly at Hana with terrifying speed.

"Midnight Sledge!"

Burst's fist rammed into Hana with a blast of raw magica and violently drove her into the pavement. The street cracked and buckled as Hana screamed in pain. Burst tucked and rolled out and sprang back to her feet in one fluid motion, as if that attack were the most effortless thing imaginable.

"Such a disappointment," she snarled as she lifted Hana up off the pavement. "Bloom was right. You're all so predictable!"

She threw Hana at Nova, who yelped in surprise just as Hana crashed into her. The two of them went flying straight through the solid brick wall of a nearby warehouse.

With Nova's concentration broken, her drum attack faded. Bloom and Blaze, now freed from their beating, took off toward Sara and Cass. I was on my own now.

I knew I needed to help Hana and Nova. Unfortunately, Burst was in my way. She grinned sinisterly, and ran at me.

"Alright, let's see what you've got, new girl!"

In the few moments I had, I fired my keytar, but Burst generated more of those magica discs and bounced between them, dodging every shot. Her speed was unreal.

She shot at me like a bullet, pulled back her fist, and shouted again.

"Darkness Burst Piledriver!"

A shaped orb of magica engulfed her fist as she slammed it into my face.

In the blink of an eye, my body crumpled into the pavement. A moment later, she was on top of me, holding me down and punching me with magica, over and over and over. *Punch. Punch. Punch.*

It was as if she was punching straight into my bones. I could feel myself getting driven deeper into the asphalt with every impact. In my panic, I did the first thing that came to mind.

I grabbed her other hand and bit her knuckles as hard as I could.

I felt something warm in my mouth; her scream confirmed it was her blood. I bit down harder, trying to distract her from pummeling me to death. For a split second, the beating stopped, which gave me an opening to smash my knee up into her gut.

With my other hand, I jabbed the neck of my keytar into her chest and smashed the keys. An atonal mess of sounds assaulted my ears, but it would have to do. I fired the resulting fizzing, sparking bolt of magica into her.

It wasn't much, but it blew her off me. I struggled up onto my knees just in time to see her stand up again, clutching her bloody fist.

She glared at me with pure, raw hatred. "What the hell! Magical girls don't bite!"

I spit the blood from my mouth. "I don't know any better! I'm the new girl!" I smashed my hands down onto the keytar and fired another, more potent bolt, knocking her off-balance again.

And that's when I heard a familiar, angry voice coming from behind her.

"She's new, but I ain't!"

A trio of glowing cymbals sliced through the air at tremendous speed and smashed the back of Burst's head, followed by the rest of a magical drum kit. With every hit, she staggered. Finally, she flopped onto the street on her stomach.

"Yeah, you like that, creep?" Nova shouted as she pulled herself and Hana from the rubble of the warehouse. "That's what you get! That's what you get when you come after Magica Riot!"

I was momentarily relieved. "Are you two okay?"

"We're hurt, but still breathing," Hana said as she gestured down the street. "I'm more concerned about Red and Yellow now."

I turned to find Cass and Blaze trading shots of supercharged magica back and forth, each dodging and weaving around the other's attacks. Blaze seemed to be able to command magica with her bare hands, and while Cass's guitar was quick and precise, Blaze was closing the gap between them.

Sara was faring no better against Bloom. Even though Sara was in top form, slicing and moving in a steady flow, Bloom countered every attack perfectly. She looked bored, like she knew Sara's next move before Sara did.

"We gotta do something, babes," Nova said. "I ain't gonna let these flammin' jerks win!"

"I agree," Hana said, "but they hit like trucks! What are we going to do?"

And then, an idea struck me, and I smiled.

"If they hit like a truck, then we need to hit like a van."

Nova stared at me as if I'd spoken Swedish. "Huh? Did ya get smacked around a little too hard, babe?"

"Just go with it," I said. "Come on, follow me!"

I took off running away from the fight, and around the corner, where I came face-to-face with Vancent Price.

I flung open the driver's door and slipped behind the wheel. "Get in!"

"You ain't making sense," Nova said.

"What are you planning, Purple?" Hana asked.

I exhaled, relieved they had actually followed me. "We have to do something they aren't expecting!"

A sudden smile of recognition flashed across Hana's face. "You're going to hit them with Vancent!"

"What?!" Nova yelped. "Babe, you can't do that to him!"

I shook my head. "It's gonna be okay! I think! I have a plan!"

Hana opened the passenger door and motioned for Nova to join her. "We won't let anything happen to him. Let's see what Purple's cooking!"

Nova pouted for a moment, then shrugged and hopped in. "Well, I guess I *am* kinda curious."

I shifted Vancent into drive and smashed the accelerator to the floor as I explained my hastily-assembled plan.

"Okay, Green, use your bass to charge Vancent with magica. Also, can you shape an energy wall into a battering ram on the nose?"

Hana grinned at me. "I can try!"

"Great! Blue, I need you to pull a trampoline again. One big enough for a van."

"Are you sayin' you're gonna launch him into the air?" Nova asked.

"That's exactly what I'm saying!"

"I have to hand it to you," Hana said, "the Menagerie will never expect that! We'll catch them by surprise!"

I nodded. "Yeah, you're getting it!"

I cranked the wheel and skidded around the corner. As I accelerated down the street, I pointed Vancent's nose directly at Bloom and just hoped that Sara would get out of the way in time.

"Alright! Green, charge up!"

Hana played a complicated bass riff, and Vancent began to glow with green magica. One of her shockwave walls formed just ahead of the hood, rippling and churning with energy.

I laughed. "Yeah, that's it! Blue, get ready! Trampoline, on my mark!"

Nova aimed her sticks out the windshield and focused on a rapidly approaching patch of pavement. The margin of error was tiny, and I had no idea if this would even work, but we were committed now.

I took a deep breath as we barreled ahead. "Okay, ready..."

Sara had told me to think for myself, to improvise. I hoped this was what she meant.

"...now, Blue!"

With a flash of light, Nova fired magica from her sticks. Two huge holo drums appeared on the pavement, and I corrected our course to bring the tires directly over them. Moments later, we hit. Vancent jolted hard, and his nose leapt off the ground, followed by the back tires.

We were airborne in a fifteen-passenger van full of charged magica, with a glittering battering ram on the nose.

Nova's eyes went wide. "Oh *flam!*"

I reached down and gripped the door handle. "Both of you, get ready to jump!"

Vancent arced through the air, flying with far more aplomb than he should have. I waited until the moment I felt our flight path reach its peak, and yanked the door open.

"Now!"

We leapt out of the van and into the air. We only had, at most, a few seconds to pull this off, but it would have to do.

As Vancent began his descent toward Bloom and Sara, I called forth my keytar and aimed at Blaze. Our stunt had drawn her attention, which I hoped would give Cass an opening to make a counterattack.

I smashed every key I could as the pavement rushed up toward me. The power of magica surged through me, and I felt the keytar charge up all the way to that limit I'd felt before.

Then, I fired, moments before I slammed into the street.

Pain shot through me. I was carrying a lot of speed, and I tumbled down the street for what seemed like an eternity as the world spun. I heard other blasts of magica going off, followed by a metallic crash.

I couldn't stop here. I had to be ready for anything that came next. With my remaining strength, I smashed my hands and feet into the pavement to stop my roll, skidding to a stop.

I was exhausted and shaky, but I forced myself to stand. Off to the side, Blaze lay slumped over on the street, while Cass helped Hana and Nova up off the sidewalk.

Vancent Price had come to a stop not far from me; his nose was pretty banged up, but he was upright and his engine still idled. Two tire tracks ran from him down the street and led me to a very surprised Sara, sitting up on the pavement after diving out of the way.

And there, in the center of those tire tracks, lay Bloom, smashed into the pavement.

I ran over and extended a hand to Sara to help her up. As she stood, she glanced at Vancent, then back to me.

"You know, I'm really impressed you took the initiative, but—how did you decide on *that?*"

I shrugged nervously. "I figured I should think big?"

She smiled and shook her head. "That one's going in the Alliance record books."

Cass ran up and wiped the sweat from her forehead. "You two okay?"

"All good," Sara said as she looked around at the three downed Menagerie girls. "We need to retrieve those devices they were using."

"Right," Cass said. "I'll grab blondie's."

"And I wanna get Burst's," Nova said. "That's what she gets for throwin' me through a wall!"

"I'll grab Bloom's," I offered.

"Stay on the alert," Sara said.

I walked over to Bloom's unconscious body. She'd fallen face-first, and her tube device was underneath her. Seeing no other alternative, I kneeled down beside her, reached out, and started to nudge her over onto her back.

That's when she snapped back to life and grabbed my wrist.

Everything in me screamed to get away, but my muscles simply didn't respond. I felt a pulse of energy shoot up through my arm and reach my heart as Bloom looked up at me. My eyes met hers, framed by her mask, and...

And they weren't red. They were purely, brilliantly blue.

The entire thing happened in a flash, but in those few heartbeats, the girl I saw wasn't the vicious, dangerous Menagerie Bloom. She was a regular girl, and it was hard to tell, but she almost looked relieved to see me.

Then, as quickly as it happened, the energy faded, and she released me. I panicked, yelped, and fell back onto the street.

"Purple, what's going on?" Sara asked.

"I ... she ..." I stammered, but I was still too rattled to get the words out.

And just a moment later, it no longer mattered, as Bloom slowly began to push herself back up onto her feet.

I scooted back and stood, then ran to Sara and Hana's side. Bloom turned to face us with a wicked sneer across her lips, framed by rivulets of blood trailing down from her nose.

Her eyes were glowing red again.

"I have to admit, new girl," she said, "I wasn't expecting you to throw a van at me. Credit where credit is due."

"How are you still standing after that?" Hana asked.

With a single fluid gesture, Bloom fired bolts of energy from her hand to Burst and Blaze, each of whom started to stand, causing Nova and Cass to back off.

"That which powers us is beyond anything you can imagine."

Sara broke away from us and stalked toward her. "Enough of this. Who are you, *really?*"

"Not yet!" Bloom snapped back at her. She stared daggers at Sara before her expression oddly softened. "It's much more fun for me if you soak in that anticipation for a little longer."

I half-expected Sara to unleash another attack right then and there, but instead, she paused, then took a halting step back.

Bloom smiled a very curious sort of smile, as Blaze and Burst joined her. "This has been a very educational experience, but I'm afraid we have to be running now."

"We can't let you do that," Cass said.

Burst laughed. "You don't have a choice."

A trio of those spinning magica discs, like the one Burst had used before, appeared beneath them. With a flash of red energy, they launched themselves off over the rooftops and out of sight.

Nova frowned up at them as they departed. "Show-offs!"

Hana touched my arm and looked at me with concern. "Are you okay, Purple? Did she hurt you when she grabbed you?"

I tried to focus, but whatever had happened before Bloom stood, the entire thing was becoming hazy and fading from my mind. It was as if I was forgetting a dream, and I suddenly began to doubt that it had even happened.

"No, I—I'm okay," I finally said.

Our wrist links beeped, and we waited a long moment for Sara to answer.

She didn't even move.

Finally, Cass raised her wrist and answered the call. "Commander, this is Riot Yellow."

While Cass handled that, Hana, Nova, and I waited for Sara to say something, *anything*.

"Boss lady? You got any, like, orders?" Nova asked.

She turned and moved her lips as if she was about to speak, but nothing came out.

"Is there something wrong?" Hana asked.

"I don't know," Sara finally said. "That girl, I—let's just get back to the Vault, okay?"

| 13 |

The sun was starting to set as we wheeled the injured Vancent Price into the hidden tunnel that led back to the Vault's garage. He was still running, technically, but he wasn't happy about it, and I felt weirdly guilty about having harmed him.

As we parked, Commander McCoy and Dr. Barrera were already waiting for us with anxious looks on their faces.

"What the hell happened out there?" the commander asked.

"They're magical girls," Hana said as we stepped out of Vancent, "but like none I've ever seen before."

Cass nodded. "They call themselves the Menagerie."

"I do *not* like them," Nova added.

The commander frowned. "The Menagerie? So you were able to communicate w—"

"We need to go after them," Sara interrupted. "They're an extreme danger."

Dr. Barrera put her hand up. "Before you do anything else, you girls are coming to the med bay for a complete examination."

"And then we're going to take the time to make a real plan," the commander added.

Sara frowned, tension plainly visible in her face, in her posture. "Commander, respectfully, the Menagerie is a clear and present—"

"*Respectfully*, Agent Ward, going off half-cocked and putting the team in further danger is not an acceptable solution. And you know it."

Sara stared back at her. She looked like a dam about to break, but eventually, she exhaled. "Understood."

* * *

Dr. Barrera insisted on giving each of us individual examinations, one at a time, in her office. Sara volunteered to go first, leaving the rest of us waiting in chairs in the corridor. Nova nestled between Hana and I, with Cass farthest away.

I figured Sara just wanted to get it over with, but the longer the examination took, the more I wondered if something else was going on. Finally, she stepped out of the office, muttering something about "fresh air." It sounded like an excuse, but the Vault's recycled air didn't exactly appeal to me, either.

I was next. Dr. Barrera poked and prodded, scanned and examined, all in a silent way that unnerved me a little.

"Is everything okay?" I managed after a few minutes.

"You seem to be holding together rather well," she said. "Your magical form is quite resilient."

"No, I mean—"

"No, it's not, but there's nothing any of us an do about it right now. I'm sorry, Claire. Maybe Sara can explain it better."

She turned away from me then, typing on her computer terminal.

"Sara likes watching the river," she added, not looking away from the screen. "You're free to go. Please tell Nova I'm ready for her."

With that, I stood and left, no more at ease than when I entered.

Outside, I tapped Nova on the shoulder. "The doctor's ready for you. I'm going to get some air."

Nova nodded soberly and shuffled past me. Part of me wanted to give her a hug, or tell her it would be okay, but I was afraid of making things more awkward.

Apparently free and with the doctor's hint fresh in my mind, I made my way up through the tunnels to the surface and emerged at Waterfront Park just as the sun was beginning to kiss the tops of the western hills. The air was warm, and the park was full of people, some jogging or cycling and some laying out on blankets on the grass.

And there, off by herself at the railing along the river, was Sara.

"Hey," I said as I approached. "You mind some company?"

She looked back and gave me a tired smile. "Not at all."

I leaned down on the railing next to her and looked out across the water. Despite the rumble of cars crossing the Burnside bridge and the occasional power boat zooming down the river, the view was rather peaceful.

"You come here a lot?" I asked.

"Yeah. Ever since I was a little kid. It was 'the big city' to me, the bridges and everything. The river seemed so powerful. I know some people get weird about Portland these days, but I've always loved this city."

I smiled. "I get it, actually. Portland always seemed like freedom to me."

"Freedom?"

"Yeah. I always daydreamed about coming out, but I was scared to do it back home. It took getting away and moving here before I really thought about it. Of course, I was still too scared. And then the Maidensong pushed me the rest of the way."

She smiled back. "The Maidensong just saw the bravery in you."

"I don't feel too brave. Nova was the one who—"

"Nova talks a good game, but she isn't really ..." She trailed off and looked out over the river. "You rescued her that night, and that took a lot of courage."

I thought back to that first night, after the Clarion Room show. "I guess the Maidensong needed me to save her."

"The Maidensong doesn't cause you to become a hero. You awakened because you wanted to save her. Because you *are* a hero. That's how it works. That's when it happens."

"Oh."

"So thank you. For saving Nova. For saving ..." She trailed off again and quietly smiled. "Just, thank you."

We spent several long moments in quiet thought, watching the river water ripple past as it flowed under the bridge.

Finally, Sara broke the silence and motioned toward a spot farther down the railing. "You know, right over there by that concrete post, that's where Iris and I first kissed."

"Really?"

She reached up and touched the lavender scarf tied around her neck. "We'd been flirting pretty shamelessly ever since the group started. After a nasty fight with Sorceress Makula's minions—"

"That's the second time I've heard you mention this Sorceress lady," I interrupted.

She laughed. "That's a really long story I'll have to tell you sometime. Anyway, after the fight, Iris and I came back here, and I just couldn't help myself."

"That must have been cute."

"It was. I was so nervous. Almost talked myself out of it. I guess I just realized that any time we go out there, one of us might not come back, so I needed to do it before it was too late." Her smile slowly vanished. "Turns out I was right, I guess. When I think about her, the empty space in my life—Claire, I just scream."

"Is that what happened at the Clarion Room?"

She nodded. "Sometimes, I don't know what else to do but let it out on stage."

I could feel the ache in her voice, and thought again about the aftermath of the fight in St. Johns. "Hey, so, what happened back there with the Menagerie? The way you reacted to Bloom..."

"Iris, when she had a secret, or like, when we were in bed, she liked to deny me, just a little. Said the anticipation made it more fun for her."

I didn't immediately make the connection, but then, it hit me. Bloom had said exactly that. Did Sara see some kind of connection between Bloom and Iris?

"That could just be a coincidence," I said.

"It could be, but it didn't feel like a coincidence to me."

"Sara, that's—"

"She knew exactly what I was going to do. *Exactly*, Claire. I couldn't land a solid hit, no matter what I tried. That wasn't luck."

I thought for a moment, scrolling back through my mental log and poring over other things Bloom and her companions had said. "When I was fighting Burst, she said Bloom called us predictable."

She frowned. "I don't know what it all means. I just know that I felt something. Something that reminded me of Iris. People have told me to move on, to accept that she's dead, but we never recovered her body. I mean, we live in a world of literal magic. I never thought it was that simple."

I looked back out over the river and tried to put the pieces together, but nothing clicked. And there was definitely no way to have a friendly chat with Bloom, so the problem seemed beyond my immediate ability to wrestle with.

The buzz of my phone derailed my train of thought. When I pulled it from my pocket, a text message from Hazel was waiting for me.

"Hey, rock star. Been working on a little something for you. Wanna come see?"

Before I could say anything, Sara broke the silence.

"I'm going to hang out here for a while," she said. She glanced at my phone and smiled. "You have plans?"

"Looks like it. Hazel wants me to come over. Do you think it's okay, with everything that's going on? I don't want to—"

"You should go, Claire," she said, looking back out across the river. "You've fought enough today. Don't fight regret, too."

***

Night was falling by the time I made it to Hazel's apartment. She opened the door with a broad, shining grin, and invited me inside.

"Can I get you anything?" she asked. "Water? Beer?"

After the day I'd had, I wasn't about to pass up a free drink. "First a beer, then a water, yeah."

"Coming right up."

I took a seat on her weathered couch, which must have been a color at one time, but now seemed too tired for such frivolity. The window behind it was cracked open, the evening breeze cooling my shoulders.

Hazel emerged from the kitchen with two bottles clutched between her fingers. She banged the caps on the edge of her table, popping them off; with her other hand, she caught the caps as they flew.

"How do you even do that?" I asked.

She handed me one of the bottles and several jigsaw pieces fell into place in my heart.

"A girl's got to have her secrets, y'know?"

"Oh, I know." I laughed nervously. "Uh, anyway, you said you had something for me?"

"I do indeed!" She took a sip from her bottle and walked over to her bookshelf, and returned with a thick white envelope. She held it out as she sat down beside me. "I wanted to give all these to you at the same time."

"All of these? What did you ..."

As I opened the flap and looked inside, I trailed off into silence as I realized what I held.

The envelope was full of photos from our session at the rose garden. There I was, posed among the flowers, framed expertly by Hazel's artistic eye, bathed in soft overcast light. Close-ups, three-quarter shots, full-body shots, abstract angles, detail shots of my eyes, my hands, a shot from behind looking out through the flowers—she really had a burst of inspiration that day. The photos were incredible.

And in them all, I looked pretty. I looked *feminine*.

I stammered as the tears welled up in my eyes. "Haze ... I ..."

"There's more," she grinned. "I developed the ones from your first show, at Cosmic Club. There's not too many of them, since it got cut short, but I wanted to get them in there!"

I flipped to the gig photos. There, too, I looked—*correct*. Like I belonged.

The tears were threatening to flow, but I fought through them. "Haze, these are amazing."

She beamed at me. "I'm just glad I got to take them."

I flipped through the photos again. "It's wild, I never knew I looked like this."

"What do you mean?"

I thought for a moment, searching for the right words. "One of the things that kept me from coming out was that I was scared I'd never look right. I'd never be pretty. Silly as that sounds."

"Hey, I can understand why you were scared." Her voice was gentle. "Beauty standards are a bunch of crap, but it's hard to make yourself believe that. You definitely don't need to worry. You seem like you were custom-made to be a girl."

"Yeah?"

"Well, yeah, Claire." She gestured at my body. "I mean, *look at you*. I've never seen hormones work that quickly."

I felt myself blushing. "Yeah, uh, it's nuts, right? I guess I just took to it really well, or something."

She giggled. "I'll say. You're gorgeous. You're practically glowing all the time! I'm so proud of you."

As the heat rushed to my cheeks and the beer tickled my brain, I slipped up just a little bit. "That means a lot coming from someone as pretty as you are."

I froze as I realized what I'd just said. Hazel sat up and leaned toward me as a mischievous grin curled across her lips.

"Why Claire, do you think I'm *pretty*?"

I gulped and looked at her. She was so soft, her sparkling eyes so kind. Of *course* I thought she was pretty. I thought she was so pretty I almost couldn't stand it. "Well, uh, I mean, I always have. I used to hope I could be as pretty and cool a girl as you someday."

She smiled at me, so warmly and genuinely that I felt like I was melting. "And now, here you are. Claire Ryland, a pretty and cool girl. I'm so glad I got to show you how I see you."

"How you ... see me?"

"Mmhmm," she nodded. "A beautiful, kind girl. It's like I told you before, I'm a lesbian. I know women. I love women. And you are one of my favorites."

I could feel myself trembling, but I tried to ignore it. "You're one of my favorites, too."

We held eye contact for much longer than seemed normal. My anxiety was raging, but there was no chance I was going to look away now. She was just *so gorgeous*, and I ...

"... ng tomorrow?"

I blinked. She'd said something, and I was so fluster-drunk that I'd zoned out. "Sorry, what did you say?"

She leaned in closer. "I said, what are you doing tomorrow?"

"Uh, I don't think I have anything planned yet. Why?"

"Because I'd like to go to the Saturday Market with you, and go get lunch, and maybe go do some other stuff."

"Oh. That sounds, um, really good, yeah. I'd like that too."

I felt like we were inching closer together, and I had no idea which of us was doing it. Was she? Was I? Were we both? She seemed close. Her eyes were so pretty. Even her smell was wonderful. She seemed *really* close. What was happening?

"Great," she smiled, "it's a date."

My heart pounded like a jackhammer. "A date?"

She was extremely close now, and reached up to brush my hair back. "Is that something you'd like, Claire?"

"Yes," I said, nodding dreamily. "Yes, definitely."

She stared straight into me, so close I could feel the air change temperature. "Good. And you know, since it's so late, you could just spend the night. With me."

It felt as if a bomb were going off in my brain. "Haze...are you saying..."

She smiled. "I'm saying, yeah. As long as it's something you want."

A thousand thoughts smashed together inside me. I'd done this before, but never as a girl. Let alone *with Hazel.* A part of me was terrified I wouldn't know what to do, that I'd be a disappointment. I was, after all, literally a new girl. How could I measure up for somebody who was already experienced?

And another, very loud part of me yearned, absolutely *ached*, to be with her.

I nodded. "It's something I want."

"So do I," she whispered. Her eyes started to close, and I felt my own closing in response.

And then, her lips touched mine.

It felt so different as a girl. Her kiss was tender, as if warm rose petals were wrapping around me. It was sweet, and new, and exciting—and underneath it all, it was also urgent, and needful, and raw.

Her hands started to roam over my body, and I sank into a blissful haze.

* * *

Quite a bit later, after we'd finished a set of activities that were new and incredible, we ended the night in Hazel's bedroom. She wrapped me up in her arms, and I nestled against her, euphoric in the warmth of her body and the glow of our mutual exploration. Gradually, we drifted off to sleep.

Suddenly, I found myself standing on a familiar industrial backstreet in St. Johns.

It was daylight again, but the city was quiet, the air hazy and still. A short distance in front of me sat Vancent Price, exactly as he'd been after our aerial stunt. I stood beside the tire tracks that marked his path after landing. Sara, Cass, Hana, and Nova where nowhere to be seen.

Slowly, I followed those tire tracks, and turned around. They extended farther back down the street, and just as before, Bloom lay face-down on the pavement between them—except now, she was not alone. Standing over her was another girl, one who looked oddly familiar.

A girl wearing my costume.

She had long brown hair that framed a rounded, kind face. Her expression was one of pity as she gazed down at Bloom, but as she looked up at me, it shifted into relief. Her eyes lit up as they met mine, radiant blue just as Bloom's had been for that brief moment when she grabbed me.

"So," she said, "you're the new Riot Purple."

"Um, yeah," I answered. "My name's Claire."

She grinned. "It looks damn good on you. I'm so glad to meet you, Claire. I'm Iris."

I froze and stared as my mouth fell slack. There was no way that could be true—and yet, I realized why she seemed familiar. I'd seen her in old band photos.

"How is that possible?" I asked. "You're—"

"Dead? No way. I had other ideas."

I shook my head. "I don't understand."

"Bloom's occupation of my body isn't as thorough as she'd hoped." She stepped around Bloom and came closer. "I don't have much time. When you knocked her out, she was weak enough for me to take control for a moment. That's when I grabbed you, and gave you a little gift. Think of this as the card that goes along with it."

Suddenly, that memory snapped back into focus. "That's right, I felt energy go into me."

She nodded. "You're carrying a package of magica. At the right time, it'll open and help lead you to the solution to this Menagerie problem."

I looked back down at Bloom. "Do you know what they're planning?"

"They're summoning Rennia," Iris said, with so much weight to the words, it felt as if I should already know who this Rennia person was.

"That must be the mistress that Bloom mentioned," I said.

Iris nodded.

I sighed. "And I'm guessing if she comes back, it'll all go south here?"

"Rennia is scary powerful," Iris frowned. "She's sealed away somewhere in dimensional prison, but if the Menagerie brings her back and she actually succeeds at her goals, it'll be much worse than 'going south' and much bigger than just Portland. It'll be real damn bad, in other words."

"Okay, so how do we stop them?"

"That, I don't know—but I think I know who does. The package I've given you is the doorway to get you there."

The weight of a hundred questions pressed down on me like an ocean, but above all, I kept coming back to one.

"Why me?"

Iris smiled again, reached out, and took my hands in hers. "Because we can always count on Riot Purple to do the right thing."

I blushed. "Thank you."

"And thank you, Claire. Just don't tell Nova I cussed." She let go and walked back over to Bloom. As she moved, the city began to fade out around her. "I think our time's almost up here."

"Will I ever get to talk to you again?"

"If all goes well." She bit her lip, the telltale glint of tears building in her eyes. "It might be a while. Could you do me a favor, when you're awake and with the other girls?"

"Of course, anything."

"Tell Sara that I knew, and the answer was going to be yes."

| 14 |

I woke up. Hazel's bedroom was empty and quiet. The soft, flat light of an overcast morning flooded in through the window. On any other day, I'd have been thinking about the weird dream I'd had.

This time, I knew that what had just happened to me was definitely not a dream.

I looked around and listened, expecting to hear Hazel in the other room, but there was only silence. Eventually, I noticed a small note on the bedside table and picked it up to read it.

Hey Claire—traded shifts at the video store so we'll have the rest of the day together for our date. Hope you slept well! There's coffee in the kitchen. I had a great time last night and can't wait for round two. Miss you already. XOXOXO Hazel

Our date. Our date *today*, to the Saturday Market.

Which meant I needed to get to the Vault as soon as possible to tell everybody about what happened with Iris, a sentence that still seemed impossible.

But then, "impossible" was a pretty regular thing in the world of magical girls.

I hopped out of bed and grabbed my clothes. With some luck, I could grab a Biketown bike, hit the Hawthorne Bridge, and get downtown pretty quickly, so I'd probably be okay on time.

I just hoped the rest of the girls didn't think I was losing my mind.

***

I found them with the commander and doctor, poring over data in the command center. After what I hoped was a comprehensible retelling, they stood in silence. I stared a hole in the floor, waiting for someone to say something.

Finally, Hana broke the silence. "So Iris is alive?"

"And trapped in her own body, while Bloom drives it around," Cass said.

"Incredible," Dr. Barrera said.

I looked up. "Um, then, you all believe me?"

"Babe, this is weird, don't get me wrong," Nova said, "but I don't plan on not believin' you anytime soon."

The commander raised her hand. "There's still somebody I need to hear from. Agent Ward?"

Sara nodded slowly. She remained quiet for a long moment before mumbling under her breath.

"I knew it."

"What was that?" the commander asked.

Sara took a deep breath and began again. "I knew she wasn't dead. It's an understatement to say this is a *lot* for me to handle, but it confirms all the feelings I got when we fought the Menagerie. I told Claire about how Bloom reminded me of Iris."

"That's right," I said.

"Given what Iris told you," she continued, "the Menagerie problem is even more serious than we thought. We can't let them bring back Rennia. That has to be our first priority, but now we have another job in front of us."

"We do," Cass agreed.

Sara stepped out of the group to face the rest of us. "It's not every day we get a second chance like this, and we're going to take it. I don't know how yet, but we're going to save the world, and we're going to save Iris. This is what magical girls do: we face the impossible with love. And I—we—love her, so we're going to find a way to bring her home, no matter how hard it is or how long it takes."

Cass smiled. "You know it. We all want to save her. It's not even a question."

"Absolutely," Hana said.

"Seriously, boss lady," Nova said. "Magica Riot never leaves a cutie behind!"

Even though I was the new girl who'd literally taken Iris's position, I had no hesitation. I smiled and gave Sara a nod. "We'll get it done."

Sara exhaled, and for just a moment, I saw her lower lip trembling. "Thank you."

"Now that that's settled," the commander said, "we need to start making a plan. Doctor, you ever heard of this Rennia woman?"

"I can't say I know that name, but then, I'm not a historian," Dr. Barrera said. "I'm going to need to coordinate with other Alliance branches that have staff for this sort of thing. Dr. Anozie at Alliance Lagos is an expert, so I'll reach out to her."

"Sounds good. Alright, in the meantime, let's see if we can—"

Suddenly, the room was bathed in red light as the Vault's emergency alarms sounded.

"Talk about bad timing," Hana said.

The commander tapped on her wrist link and brought up the alert on the big screen.

LARGE-SCALE PANDORA CORRUPTION INCURSION DETECTED.

"Looks like we've got a big Pandora infestation brewing," she said. A few taps more brought up a map. "Out in ... Gresham?"

"Never seen big activity that far out," Cass said.

"Same here, or such a big reading in broad daylight," Hana said. "It's near Mt. Hood Community College."

"Alright, let's pick this talk up later," the commander said. "You girls roll out, and be prepared for anything. We don't know if this is connected to the Menagerie, but assume the worst."

"Right," Sara said. "Everybody, let's get to Vancent. Saoirse fixed him up for us."

As we filed out of the command center, I tugged Sara's sleeve and pulled her aside. "Um, before we go—"

"You don't have to ask," Sara said. "I want you to know that bringing Iris back doesn't mean you're being replaced. You're a part of this family now, and you're a member of Magica Riot for as long as you want to be."

"Oh, no, I wasn't worried about that, but I appreciate it, for real."

Sara seemed genuinely relieved for a moment before regaining her usual composure. "In that case, what did you need?"

"Iris asked me to tell you something."

Her eyes widened, and I swore I saw the faintest hint of a blush in her cheeks. "She did? What did she say?"

"That she knew, and the answer would have been yes. Does that mean anything to you?"

She looked away as a private, shining smile crossed her face. "Yeah, it means a lot. A whole lot."

***

The ride down the interstate to Gresham was quiet, the five of us silent under our worries. I sat in the middle row with Sara and

Cass while Hana drove. As we neared the college, I felt Sara's hand reach out and rest on mine.

Our eyes met in the dim interior, and she gave me a subtle nod as she mouthed the words "thank you."

I smiled back, just as I felt Vancent start to slow down.

Hana called back over her shoulder at us. "We've almost reached the coordinates."

Beside her, Nova gave us a thumbs-up. "Time to bust some jerks!"

We rolled into a parking lot across the street from the college campus and brought Vancent to a halt. Ahead of us, a movie multiplex stretched out along the block. Other than the people coming and going from its entrance, there was no activity to be seen.

"Uh, is this the right place?" Cass asked.

Hana glanced at her wrist link. "This is exactly the place, according to the sensors."

"Ain't there supposed to be, like, a bunch of Pandoras here?" Nova asked.

I peered out of the windows. None of the people milling around had the telltale appearance of disguised Pandora creatures. "Maybe they're in the theater?"

Sara tapped her link. "Local scan says it's coming from the back of the building. Let's go take a look. Stay on your guard."

We got out and made our way over to the back of the building. Slowly, we moved around the corner—and found ourselves facing a very unremarkable dumpster, and nothing else.

"Alright, for real, what is going on here?" Cass asked.

Hana looked down at her wrist link and frowned. "The scans don't make sense. Nova, Claire, can you do me a favor? Go into your links and connect to mine, then stand at the corners of the building. I need to triangulate this."

Nova and I tapped the scan connection button on our links and stood where we were instructed. The air between us was tense.

"Anything yet?" Sara asked.

Hana began to zigzag slowly forward, her eyes glued to her link. "Just eliminating variables. One sec."

Something about this was extremely weird, and I started to feel ill in the pit of my stomach. The scans said there should be an absolute horde of Pandora creatures here. But what...

Eventually, Hana stopped directly in front of the dumpster.

Sara nodded, and shot the rest of us a look. "Defensive positions."

We stood in a semi-circle around the dumpster, ready to transform. My heart was thumping away, and as Sara and Hana reached for the dumpster's lid, I held my breath.

"On three," Hana said to Sara. "One, two, *three!*"

They flung open the lid. Inside lay a truly gruesome sight: a night's worth of movie theater garbage.

But that was all.

"Can Pandoras fit in trash bags?" Nova asked.

"I'm going diving," Hana said. "Watch my back."

She reached into the dumpster and pulled out a garbage bag, and another, and another. As she leaned in deeper and grabbed at more trash, she froze. An eerie red glow illuminated her features, and her expression grew confused.

"What in the world—well, I think I found the source of the readings."

"What is it?" Sara asked.

Hana reached in and pulled out a small metallic box. Most of its sides were covered with complicated circuitry, but from one side, a mound of glowing red crystals sprouted several inches outward. I recognized them immediately. I'd seen them plenty of times in the armory back at the Vault.

Thaumatite.

Hana held her link up to the box and scanned. "The readings are all coming from this device. It's blasting out a powerful signal."

"What kind of signal?" I asked.

She turned back to the rest of us and frowned. "A perfect recreation of Pandora Corruption energy signatures."

"What the flam's it for, though?" Nova asked. "Some kind of Pandora communicator?"

Hana stared at the device, and slowly, her expression soured. "I don't think it's a Pandora device."

Sara tapped open a comm line on her link. "Commander, this is Ward. We have the source of the signal."

The commander's voice replied, crackling and full of distortion. *"What is the signal source? We don't see a ch—"*

The sound cut out suddenly, and Sara tapped her link again, over and over. "Commander? Commander? Do you read?"

I checked my own link and tried to open a channel, but I was met with an angry red error message: CONNECTION INTERRUPTED. UNABLE TO PING CENTRAL SERVER.

"Hana," I said, as the feeling in my stomach curdled into dread, "what is that thing?"

Hana looked at us, and I saw a sinking realization in her eyes. "It's a decoy."

"Wait, no," Nova said. "No, no, no, that means—"

"This was a trap," Sara growled, "and we took the bait."

* * *

Sara drove us back; in her hands, Vancent Price was a missile, careening through Portland at the edge of control. A steady rain had settled in, and the interior felt very small, the five of us wound over-tight.

Nova kept shaking her head, and I could see her trembling.

"This ain't happening... this ain't happening... there's no flammin' way..."

I reached out and touched her shoulder. "Hey, c'mon, we're going to get there and—"

"What if we get there too late, babe?" she shot back. I'd never seen her so scared before; the usual unstoppable cheer on her face had fallen away, and in its place, I saw the scared young girl in the woods that she'd talked about at the band dinner. "What if the doc or the big boss or Saoirse are hurt, or worse?"

"We're going to do everything we can to make sure that doesn't happen," Hana said.

Nova's lip trembled. "But what if we ain't able to? They're *family*. These jerks can't take more family! I—I can't do that again, no way."

I slid close and put my arm around her. "We can save them. I know we can. You remember what you said to me the night we met?"

Nova sniffled. "I said a lot of stuff that night."

"Yeah, you did," I laughed. "You told me to feel your rhythm and take the lead. We're going to do that again. Give me a rhythm, and let me take the lead. We'll help them together."

I felt her head fall against my shoulder. "Okay. Okay, yeah, we will. Uh... thanks, babe. Sorry I got scared."

"We're all scared," I said as I gave her a squeeze. "I'm terrified. Nothing wrong with that. You help me, I help you."

From the front seat, Sara called back to us. "Coming up on the tunnel. Hold on. This might be rough."

I looked out through the windshield, waiting for Sara to slow down.

She did not slow down.

Vancent leapt down the tunnel at high speed, and we slid around the curving passage and came upon the security doors.

They were partially open; Sara threaded Vancent between them, and as we soared past, the left door scraped along Vancent's body with a sickening screech.

Sara aimed at Vancent's parking spot and slammed on the brakes. The tires locked up, and we skidded to a stop only inches from the wall.

"Everybody out," she said. "And be ready for anything."

We got out of Vancent and headed for the door into the Vault itself. Sara placed her hand on the handle, took a deep breath, and slid it open.

The long corridor beyond was dark, lit only intermittently by flickering lights. Somewhere deeper in the facility, the sound of magica blasts echoed against the walls. The situation was active, and volatile.

And those magica blasts all but confirmed the Menagerie was responsible.

"We're in for a fight," Cass said.

"We are," Sara agreed. "No hesitation. It's time we went to work."

She raised her hand and called down her microphone. I swallowed my nerves as the rest of us joined her.

"Maidensong harmony power ... go live!"

We transformed and took off down the corridor. The percussive blasts of magica grew louder. Near the main facilities, blast marks began to appear on the walls.

As we got closer to the armory, we found patches of blood on the floor. It didn't take long to find their source.

Saoirse lay on the corridor floor, propped up against the wall. Blood ran from cuts and scrapes on her face and stained a bandage around her left leg. Dr. Barrera, herself banged up and streaked with blood, kneeled beside her and tended to her injuries from a doctor's bag.

"Doctor, Saoirse," Sara said, "are you alright? What happened?"

"I'll be fine," Dr. Barrera said, "and Saoirse is stable, yes. It's the Menagerie. They're here."

Saoirse looked like she was about to unleash a torrent of curse words, but she glanced up at Nova and caught herself, mumbling them under her breath instead.

Cass looked down the corridor. "What's the situation?"

"They flew right past the security systems like they didn't exist," Dr. Barrera said. "Two of them went for the command center."

Saoirse gestured toward the armory door down the hall. "And the purple-haired one busted into my armory like she owned the place. Tried to hold her off, but without magica it's basically just me swingin' a plain guitar at a freight train."

"Have they gotten into the command center yet?" Hana asked.

"It all happened so bleedin' fast. I didn't have time to go into lockdown, but the big boss, she sealed everything up down there."

"I think it's just going to slow them down, not fully stop them," Dr. Barrera said.

Nova grumbled and growled. "We can't let them get in there!"

"That would be extraordinarily bad," Hana agreed. "They'd be close to accessing our computers, the citywide sensor grid, maybe even the global Alliance network."

"Aye, and there's no telling what the purple one's up to in the armory," Saoirse said.

Cass looked back to Sara. "No good options here, boss."

"No good options," Sara agreed, "which means we just have to pick one of the bad ones. Yellow, Green, Blue, can you go engage Blaze and Burst? Do whatever it takes to keep them out of the command room. Hit 'em hard."

"That, we can do," Cass said.

Nova frowned. "You gonna be okay dealing with Bloom, boss lady? You know, on account of all that stuff we learned about her?"

"It has to be me," Sara said. "Well, me and Purple."

"Wha—me too?" I asked.

"You're the only one of us who's talked to Iris for two years, and I was her girlfriend. If anybody can have an effect on her through Bloom's influence, it's us."

I couldn't argue with that logic. "Okay, yeah. Let's do it."

Cass nodded as she, Hana, and Nova called forth their instruments. "We're on it. Good luck, you two."

"Same to you," Sara said.

The three of them turned and ran off into the flickering darkness of the corridor as Sara and I made for the Armory.

As we ran, Sara reached down and grabbed my hand. "Stick with me, okay, Claire? This is going to be hard."

I smiled and squeezed back. "I've got you, I promise."

We reached the armory and peered in through the door. The room was a mess. Equipment had been tossed around in the fight, and a trail of Saoirse's blood was clearly visible. Bloom stood at the back of the room, trying to access one of the decommissioned instrument lockboxes.

The one holding Iris's keytar.

"She's trying to arm herself," I said.

Sara nodded. "Let's intervene, shall we?"

We ran in through the door and stood between Bloom and the exit. She couldn't get away without going through us, one way or another.

"Hold it," Sara called out to her. "Step away from that lockbox!"

Bloom paused, looked back over her shoulder, and grinned at us before resuming her efforts at the security lock. "No, I don't think I'm gonna do that."

I took a deep breath and stepped forward. "We don't want to hurt you!"

She laughed. "Oh Claire, I don't see a van around here, so I don't think you *can* hurt me."

Sara slowly moved forward. "It doesn't have to be like this. We know about Iris."

"You've got somebody else's body, and you're not alone in it," I said.

"You're right about one thing," Bloom said. "I'm not alone in here. My brilliance and drive have been grinding up against an irritant named Iris Carr."

There it was. "So Iris is having an effect on you."

"It wasn't supposed to be like this," Bloom continued. "When Mistress Rennia created me and placed me in this body, my takeover was supposed to be complete. Alas, Iris wasn't as dead as we thought. This is such a capable body, but it's difficult to keep her quiet." She paused and looked back at me. "At least, since she had that little heart-to-heart with you. Thank you very much for *that*."

"I can imagine it's hard," Sara said. "Iris is strong. She never knew how to stop fighting. If you stand down, we might be able to find a way to separate you."

"I don't think that's in the cards," Bloom said. "I have a job to do, and I never leave a job half-finished, for better or worse."

"Iris always used to say that, too. You're starting to sound more like her."

"Nice try, Sara. You know nothing about me. I'm not her. I'm my own person."

I took another step closer. "That's right, you are. *Your own person.* You're not like you were before."

Bloom turned and glared at us. "Shut up, Claire! I'll show you what I am!" She reached back and pressed one last button, and with a series of heavy metallic clicks and clanks, the lockbox door swung open.

"Purple ..." Sara said, dropping into a defensive posture.

I nodded and tensed my muscles, ready to move.

Bloom grabbed the old keytar and cradled it in her arms, then slipped the strap over her shoulders. She closed her eyes as the keytar surged back to life, magica glowing from within.

She opened her eyes and her mask de-materialized, finally revealing the unmistakeable face of Iris beneath it. "You could barely stop me before, and I wasn't even armed. What chance do you think you have now? While I'm helping Rennia conquer the Maidensong, your corpses will be down here, forgotten to history."

Sara stared her down and called forth her guitar. "We don't have to do this. You *can't* want to destroy the world. I know that somewhere inside you, you can hear Iris's voice telling you this is wrong."

"It doesn't matter what Iris wants, and it doesn't matter what I want!" There was a resigned edge to her voice. "All that matters is what Mistress wants! And unless you step aside and let me leave, this is how it has to be!"

Sara did not step aside. "Have it your way. Purple, let's give her a show."

I called my keytar. Without Cass, Hana, and Nova, we had to act quickly—and the perfect song popped into my head.

I took a deep breath and played the opening riff of "Like You."

Sara glanced at me and started to strum the song's chords. I switched to playing Hana's bass part to give us some rhythm and felt the magica in our instruments start to harmonize and boost each other.

While Sara transitioned into the first verse, Bloom leapt at us, her keytar held aloft like a war hammer. She smashed it down at Sara, who parried the attack as magica crackled through the air. Bloom snarled and pivoted toward me.

I swung my keytar up to deflect her next blow, which landed with the force of a hurricane. Bloom's strength was overwhelming, fueled by the rage of her corruption energy and the magica she was stealing from Iris. She was on another level from Burst; my muscles screamed in fire as I pushed back against the assault and the limits of my own power.

Bloom lunged at us again. I blocked, giving Sara an opening to swing her guitar at Bloom's torso, but Bloom adjusted mid-swing to knock the guitar away with a downward swoop. She pressed her new advantage, jabbing and slicing at us, snarling with increasing agitation as Sara and I kept pace with her.

The onslaught was relentless. I already felt exhausted and battered, but I forced myself to keep going as Sara pushed her way through into the chorus. With a stroke of luck, we blocked one of Bloom's attacks, and our three instruments clashed together in a chaotic blast of magica that briefly knocked her back and gave us an opening.

Sara lunged forward, slicing away as she sang.

"What's it like to be like you? What's it like to be beautiful and true?"

Bloom glared and raged at us. "Shut your mouth! Stop singing that damn song!"

I jabbed in with my keytar. "Are you mad at us, or are you mad because hearing Iris's lyrics makes you feel her emotions?"

"SHUT UP!"

"YOU FIRST!" Sara snarled. "Iris is full of love, and kindness, and anxiety, and pain, and joy—and now you have to handle it! Look at me, and feel what Iris felt for me, and deal with it! Your mistress can never give you that!"

Bloom suddenly lurched backward, groaning. She clutched her head in both hands. A rivulet of blood trickled down from her nose, and her face wrenched into pain and confusion.

"Stop it! Stop doing this to me! I will not betray Mistress Rennia! The plan begins today!"

"You can be free if you just stand down!" Sara shouted back. "We can—"

"I *can't!*" Bloom snapped. She slammed her hand down onto the keys of her keytar and aimed it at Sara as it glowed a fiery red with overcharged, corrupted magica.

With terrifying speed, she jabbed the keytar's neck into Sara's chest. Sara screamed, loudly and piercing; Bloom's face twisted in response to some deep pain, and for a moment, she flinched.

"Please," Sara whispered. "Iris..."

Bloom fired.

Sara flew back and slammed into the armory's wall with a sickening thud. I tried to react, to swing my own keytar at Bloom, but she was far too quick.

She roared, and the last thing I remembered was the body of her keytar, glowing with magica, swinging directly into my chest.

* * *

I regained consciousness in the medical bay. Dr. Barrera stood above me, bloodied and bruised, but alive. It took me a moment to realize I must be alive, too.

She smiled softly. "Welcome back, Claire."

"How long was I out?"

"Not long this time. Minutes. A fair sight better than the day we met. You're going to be okay. In fact, if you'd like to sit up, we all have some urgent business to discuss."

I groaned and pushed up on my elbows to find the rest of the band and Commander McCoy standing nearby. The band looked exhausted and listless, while the commander—bandages around her chest and her left arm in a sling—somehow managed an attentive stance.

I was just relieved to see Sara and the other girls alive and standing, as rough as they looked.

"Alright, that's everybody," the commander said. "Very glad to see you awake again, Claire."

Nova's face lit up as she saw me, and she bounded across the floor to wrap me up in a hug. Up close, I could tell she'd been crying. "Don't you ever scare me like that again, babe!"

I hugged her back. "I'll try not to. What happened?"

"The Menagerie escaped," Sara said. "Once Bloom knocked us out cold, they just brute-forced their way back out."

"Seems like they got what they came for," Cass added.

"When they reached the computers, they accessed one thing," the commander said. "The data frequency of the Alliance's Portland sensor network."

"What can they do with that?" I asked.

Hana shrugged. "Not much, other than jamming the signal. But the network is so heavily redundant that they couldn't take it all out. The only way you could disrupt it is with an interference source so big, we probably wouldn't need the sensors to find it anyway."

Cass nodded. "It doesn't add up. We know they're trying to bring back this Mistress Rennia person. How do the sensors connect to that?"

"That's the million-dollar question," the commander said. "And we're just about outta guesses."

"We need something more to work with," Sara said. "Claire, I don't suppose Iris's magical zip file has done anything yet?"

I shook my head. "Not a thing. All she said was it'd open when the time was right. But considering what Bloom said, time isn't really on our side."

Hana's eyebrows shot up. "Wait, what did Bloom say?"

"Right before she knocked us out, she said 'the plan begins today.'"

"It's almost noon," Cass said. "This could be about to go down."

Nova frowned. "This is super-duper not good."

"Agreed," the commander said. "The entire city is in danger. I've going to talk to the Alliance, figure something out. This is as bad as it's been in a long time."

"Is there any kind of plan for something like this?" Hana asked.

"Until we know what we're dealing with, we don't know what to plan for," the commander explained. "Right now, we only have one play left in the playbook. We deal with this, quick and quietly. If it goes belly-up, we improvise."

I felt my phone buzz in my pocket, and pulled it out to check the text message notification on the screen. It was from Hazel.

Heya, rock star. I'm here!

"Oh no oh no oh no oh no," I said, as I felt the blood drain from my face. Portland might be on the edge of turning into a dimensional war zone, and my girlfriend had just walked into the middle of it.

"What's wrong?" Sara asked.

"Hazel. She's here. At the Saturday Market."

Sara grabbed my shoulder. "You've got to get her out of here. Out of downtown, out of Portland. However you can."

Panic rose up inside me. "I—but we still have to—"

"Claire, *go*. This problem will still be here. Go help her. Don't fight regret, remember?"

I looked around the room. The rest of the girls, the commander, and Dr. Barrera all nodded in affirmation.

"Alright," I said. "I'll be back."

* * *

I spotted Hazel as soon as I came up from the tunnels under the Burnside Bridge and made a beeline for her through the crowds of the market and the slow, steady Portland rain. She grinned and waved at me when she spotted me, but her expression fell to concern as she got a better look.

"Claire? Are you okay? You look like you've been in a fight!"

I ignored the question. "Haze, you've got to get out of here."

"Get out of here? What for? What's going on?"

"Something bad is happening today, and you can't be anywhere near downtown."

She shook her head. "Slow down. What bad thing?"

"I can't tell you exactly. You just have to believe me. Please, Haze, it's serious."

"Claire, are you okay? You're acting really weird."

"I know I am! You just have to trust me! It's not safe here, and—"

An all-too-familiar voice off to my right came crashing into the conversation, and my blood ran cold. "That your girlfriend, Claire?"

Bloom stood just barely past arm's reach, staring at me with those glowing red eyes, grinning wickedly like she'd just spotted her prey. Surprisingly, she was in street clothes; I didn't know the Menagerie girls could transform, but even disguised, she was menacing.

Hazel turned and looked at her. "Who are you?"

"Oh, I'm a good friend of Claire's. Isn't that right?"

I leapt in between her and Hazel. "Leave her alone."

"Why, I'm not here to cause trouble for you, specifically," Bloom said. "Not yet. As you know, I was just in the neighborhood, and thought I'd chat for a bit, one-on-one. Our last hangout ended so abruptly, after all."

"I was there, yeah."

"This is such a beautiful part of town, don't you think? Could stand a little redecoration. A bit like your sad little underground tin can did."

"What do you want?" I snapped.

Bloom stared into me. "As much fun as I had earlier today, I wanted to look you in the eyes one last time, before we upend your entire existence."

"You're going to be very sorry," I shot back. "If you hurt anyone in this city, I swear I'll—"

"Hurt? No, Claire. We're freeing them. A few eggs will get broken in the process, but that's simply the way the world works. Acceptable losses and all that."

I glared at her and felt fire in my blood. "You're a monster."

"The insults of the doomed don't interest me. Our preparations are complete. You are mere heartbeats away from the dawn of a new age—one that, I'm sorry to say, you won't live to witness."

"Claire, who is this?" Hazel asked. "She looks familiar. Kinda like—"

"She was Iris," I said, "from Magica Riot."

Hazel's jaw dropped. "What the fuck? Iris is alive?!"

"That's complicated." I stared at Bloom. "Bloom here isn't Iris. She's just squatting in Iris's body."

"Shut up, Claire," Bloom snapped back. "I think I'm putting her body to rather good use, actually. If not for you and your redheaded friend stirring her up, I'd be quite happy here indeed. If you'd just stop trying to get under my skin, I would ... I ... I would ..."

She trailed off, groaned, and suddenly grabbed the side of her head, just as she had during the fight. She winced in pain and staggered a few feet back from us.

"Shut up, shut up, *shut up!*" she shouted. A few people in the nearby crowds were starting to stare. "Stop singing that song!"

"I don't hear anything," Hazel said. "Claire, what is all this?"

"Iris is fighting back," I said.

"Oh," Hazel said, quieter. She took my hand.

I stepped toward Bloom. "You're having trouble again, huh, Bloom? I hope Iris never gives you a moment's peace."

Bloom's nose started to bleed again, and she laughed. "She's becoming quite the pest. Won't stop singing that song you two played today. Filling my head with all sorts of thoughts, feelings—and she's only getting louder. Do you have any idea how agonizing it is to live with someone's conscience nagging away at you as you try to get things done?"

"It's a normal part of being human. Maybe you'll learn something, do some growing." Another thought occurred to me, and I smiled. "Maybe it's already happening. I mean, you haven't even mentioned Rennia once in this conversation."

"Shut your mouth. *Of course* I'm thinking about Mistress. She—she's my entire reason for existence."

"Could have fooled me."

Bloom glared at me, seething. This was getting to her. "Whatever. Once Mistress is free, she'll fix me. She has to. "

"Who are you trying to convince, Bloom?"

"You are very annoying, Claire Ryland, and I promise you I'll make the short remainder of your life deeply unpleasant. At least I can take a small measure of joy knowing that you've got a front-row seat to your own annihilation."

She stepped back from me and raised her hand. A wild swirling glow of crimson light shot up around her and gradually faded away, revealing her full Menagerie form. A disc of magica appeared beneath her feet. It spun up, glowed, and a moment later, launched her in a skyward arc over the treetops of the park.

I stood there in shock as chaos erupted around me. People who had been going about their day, minding their own business and enjoying the market, gasped and shouted and pointed and yelled in mass confusion.

"What was that?"

"Did you see that?"

"The hell just happened?"

"Was that real?"

"Claire," Hazel asked, her voice still small, "what just happened?"

"Haze, it's ... it's hard to ... I don't ..." I stammered, but I truly couldn't coherently string words together at that moment. Bloom had just crashed through the secrecy of magical girls in broad daylight.

My link began to chime with a call. Dazed and operating on muscle memory, I raised my wrist and tapped the screen.

"Hi. This is Claire."

"Claire, did something happen up there in the park?" Sara asked. "The sensor grid just lit up like a Christmas tree."

"Uh, yeah, you could say that."

Hazel stepped closer to me, looking down at my link. "Claire, what is going on? Who's that?"

I stared back at her. "That's Sara."

"Sara Ward? From the band?"

"Well ... kind of?"

Sara continued, her voice becoming increasingly tense. *"Commander McCoy's on the line with Tokyo HQ. The rest of us are on our way up. Don't move!"*

I opened my mouth to tell her I wasn't planning to, but the only thing that I managed to get out was a wet croak as an intense jolt radiated out from my chest, coursing through the rest of my body.

I was only vaguely aware of the events that followed. A glow in my chest. My legs giving out. The pavement rushing up toward me. Hazel, screaming for help. I couldn't make out any words, though. My hearing was closing in around me, muffled into silence like a song fading into the distance. I felt the sensation of falling again, far past the ground in the park, into some massive, empty space, and then, everything went black.

PART THREE

Harmony

| 15 |

I woke slowly; my sense of touch returned first, but my situation became no clearer for it. The ground felt smooth, almost luxuriously so, but grippy and cool to the touch. I'd never felt anything like it before.

Around the moment I thought to try, I found I could open my eyes. Above me, massive towers shot into the sky, glittering and glowing in sunlight like they were made of crystal. As I examined them further, I realized they actually *were* crystal, a forest of crystalline architecture humming very gently. I couldn't tell how loud it was; I wasn't sure if my hearing was back or not. But it felt like a low, gentle thrum that reverberated and modulated between the variously sized crystal buildings.

Harmonizing.

I stood and took stock of my surroundings as my senses slowly returned to me. Wherever this place was, it was identifiable as a city of some sort. The general form of things slotted into a recognizable pattern: buildings lining a street.

And at the end of that street lay a grand plaza, circled by a body of water with a single, colossal skyscraper at its heart.

That central tower rose in a gently arcing swoop of crystal and metallic supports to a dramatic, needle-like spire. Near the top, a terrace jutted from the tower, and a soft prismatic rainbow light glowed from within.

That light felt strangely comforting and familiar. It also seemed to be my only lead, so the path ahead was obvious.

I began walking toward the tower. My breathing and footsteps seemed to be making music; as I moved between the buildings, they gently resonated in tune. The city was attuned to me, like a metropolis-sized orchestra to a conductor.

Those buildings were even more otherworldly than I thought, their crystalline shapes a mixture of natural growth and intricate hand-carved details. Elegant arched doors and windows covered by geometric crystal lattice gleamed as light refracted through them, the interiors beyond a mystery.

I reached the plaza and crossed a bridge to the base of the tower. Enormous arches that seemed grown from single hunks of crystal soared above me and beckoned me inside.

The interior of the tower's ground floor was vast, and empty, apart from a series of glittering tubes in the center that shot up into the ceiling and, presumably, unknown points beyond. I approached the closest; it was large enough for multiple people to stand in, and reminded me of some fantastic version of a glass elevator.

A feeling only reenforced when it lit up with a soft glow, as if to invite me inside.

At this point, I'd come too far to turn back. I decided to take it on faith that this was safe, and stepped into the tube.

There were no buttons, no obvious controls at all. I stood there for a moment and considered my situation. It would have been darkly comedic if I'd come all this way only to get stuck with a broken elevator.

A moment later, the floor of the tube came alive.

Below my feet, a ring of white light formed, followed by complex, geometric sigils of white and purple. Those sigils started to slowly spin in opposite directions as the glow became more intense, and I realized what I was seeing: this was magica, similar to the discs that let the Menagerie girls soar through the air, but far more beautiful and intricate.

The sigil ring began to rise, carrying me gently along with it. This *was* a magica-powered elevator; I rose up through the tube with increasing speed, and soon passed into darkness as I reached the lobby's ceiling.

Then, suddenly, I emerged into daylight, and was greeted by an astonishing view. The crystal city stretched out below me as I swept up along the tower. It was incredibly dense, miles across, and completely circular. Beyond its edge lay only water.

This was a giant circular crystal city floating in the ocean.

As the elevator slowed, I was struck by an odd sense of familiarity, as if a part of me knew this place. It felt like a foggy, distant memory from another time.

I came to a stop at the terrace level near the top of the tower and took a deep breath. Whatever lay inside, I had no choice but to confront it. I turned and stepped out of the tube, into the space beyond.

The room had a gentle, cozy feel. Soft curtains hung from pink crystal walls. A plush-looking bed occupied one corner. Outside, on the terrace, stood a dining table and chairs among lush planters filled with purple, pink, and white roses. A space resembling a kitchen took up the wall across from the elevator.

Standing at what must have been a countertop next to what I understood to be a stove, a woman was making tea. She wore an opalescent white and gold dress, its sun-bright gleam contrasting with the warm jasper of her skin. The dress shimmered, as if in surprise, as the woman noticed me and turned.

She smiled and waved. "Please come in, Miss Claire. I won't be a moment! Make yourself at home!"

Before I could answer the mysterious woman, the ringing of a kitchen timer cut through the distance between us, and she beamed in delight.

"Oh, good, it's done steeping. Claire, why don't you head out to the terrace? I'll bring this right over for you."

She turned back to her kitchen. I could think of no better options, so I took her up on that idea and walked through the room out into the sun.

I followed the gently curving wall of rose planters as I slowly navigated the terrace. Far below me, the crystal city glimmered in the light, the ocean beyond an endless blue. I took my time, letting my sightseeing cover for my thoughts.

Whoever she was, the woman seemed friendly. That could be a trap, but I got the feeling if she'd wanted me dead, she wouldn't be going to all this trouble.

That still didn't answer the question of her identity. Was *this* the person Iris said would know how to stop the Menagerie?

The *clink* of mugs being set down on a table drew my attention back to her, as she took a seat and motioned for me to join her.

I paused. "Can you tell me where I am?"

She picked up her mug and took a long sip before answering. "Technically, this is a recreation of home. A great distance from where you came, long ago, and far off in the future."

"I don't know what that means."

"I know. Come, join me, before the tea gets cold. Our time is, unfortunately, limited."

I walked back to the table and sat down in the chair across from her. "So, who are you? Are you, like, a god? An alien? Something I'm dreaming up after a head injury?"

She laughed. "Miss Claire, I can promise you I'm not a dream, or an alien."

"That doesn't cover 'god,' though."

"Nor does it cover 'head injury.'" She smiled gently and flourished with her hand. "The concept of gods was something created to explain memories stored deep inside the human heart. I wouldn't use that term for myself."

"Okay, noted. So who *are* you?"

She took another long sip of tea. "That isn't the most pressing matter right now. Your world is about to irreversibly change, Miss Claire."

"You're talking about the Menagerie, and Rennia."

She nodded. "Your world line is headed toward a major shift, a decision point. If Rennia is freed, she will connect to the Maidensong, corrupting it." Another long sip. "One way or another, the world enters a new era today. It's up to you and your fellow maidens to decide what kind of era it's going to be."

"That's a pretty big thing to wrap my head around." I sighed. I brought my own mug to my lips and took a drink, letting the warm, floral taste wash over me. "It sounds like you're saying we have to change the world."

"That is exactly what I'm saying, Miss Claire."

I shook my head. "How are we supposed to do that?"

Her eyes met mine, and she smiled. "You must access your true power."

"Our true power?"

She put her mug down and leaned closer. "You've felt it before, haven't you? How there is something beyond your reach, beyond your current ability. Something you can't access, but which calls to you."

"Yeah, more than once. Cass and Hana called it 'the wall.' Said nobody could go past it."

"They're correct, but it was not always so." A wistful, emotional expression crossed her face. "Magical girls were not always a secret. They operated openly as humanity's champions, and had access to truly staggering abilities they used to craft a world of equity and kindness, a world free from want. All that was lost as a consequence of the original incident with Rennia, a long time ago."

"And getting that back is how we stop her?"

"Correct. Your predecessor Iris gave you a gift, and now I get to put the finishing touches on it for her. When you next transform, it will tell the Maidensong to unlock that power. That is how you will save the world, and how you will change it. How you will remake society to show the world a better way. Simply put, our day of rebirth has arrived."

I looked away as I spiraled through the implications of what she was saying. When I'd talked to Iris, I had no idea that I'd be suddenly faced with the prospect of a challenge this massive. Stopping the Menagerie wouldn't be a simple matter of preventing them from carrying out their plan; it would involving changing the *entire world*, a task I had no confidence in myself to accomplish.

What qualifications did I have to alter the course of the planet's history? Why was the fate of humanity itself being handed to me, someone who hadn't even been out as a girl for more than a month?

"I don't know if I can do this," I said quietly.

"I do." She smiled. "You had the bravery to live, to fight, to *become* Claire Ryland. That bravery, and your genuine kindness, is why the Maidensong chose you to become Riot Purple."

"But I barely know what I'm doing, as a girl *or* a magical girl."

"You're not doing this alone." She reached across the table and took my hand. Her touch was warm in a way that went beyond physical temperature; even from this small connection, I could feel the tremendous amount of magica in her. "I know you're scared, but you are not the one fated hero. Despite what stories might say, that isn't the way the world works."

"Then somebody else, somebody like Sara, has the experience that—"

"You *have* Sara's experience, and Cass's determination, and Hana's clarity, and Nova's enthusiasm. And they have you, Claire. The fact that you are all magical girls means you have what it takes to do this. Nobody is alone, nobody the sole author of their lives. Change takes people working together, and together, you girls will change the world today."

I sat back and slowly wrung my hands together as I tried to tame the anxiety that was raging inside me. This was so much to take at once. I shouldn't be the one making this kind of decision. I wasn't ready for this, wasn't ready for the respon—

"Claire," the woman said as she squeezed my hand harder.

"Y-yeah?"

"You can do this. Think back to the night of your awakening."

"My awakening?"

"Remember how you felt then? That feeling of power and confidence?"

"Well, yeah, but—"

"You hadn't started to second-guess yourself. That power is inside of you. Combine it with the true power of the Maidensong and let it shine out into the world again."

"But I've barely gotten the hang of my *current* powers. How am I supposed to deal with a whole new set?"

"You already know how to use them. As a magical girl, they are a part of you. You simply need to have your full connection to the Maidensong restored. They will come back to you."

In other words, I was going to have to take it on faith. "Well, okay. I'll try my best."

"I know you will. Use your power for good, to help people. And, if you come up against something too dangerous to defeat, listen for the Exalted Harmony. It will carry you to victory."

"The Exalted Harmony? What's that?"

The woman sighed and let go of my hand. "Unfortunately, my dear, our time is up."

My sense of hearing closed in on me. The edges of my vision darkened and blurred, and the room stretched away from me as the void took me once again.

***

A moment later, I heard muffled voices. My back was against something hard and rough, while cool wet splatters peppered my face. Indistinct blobs of light swirled in front of me as my head spun. Sparkling zaps of magica popped all over my body.

Slowly, those muffled voices became more distinct and recognizable.

"What happened to her?" Sara asked.

Hazel's voice replied. She sounded panicked and urgent, like she'd been crying. "I don't know! She was just talking to that girl who flew away, and then you called, and then she fell."

"She doesn't seem to be bleeding," Hana said.

"You think Iris's package finally opened?" Cass asked.

"We gotta do something," Nova said. "She looks so pale and sick!"

"I don't understand," Hazel said. "What's going on? How did that girl do all that?"

"That ... complicated," Sara said.

Suddenly, everything snapped back into focus again. I sat bolt upright, gasping for breath, my eyes wide. Rivulets of rain slid down my face as my senses recovered from the shock.

Sara grabbed my shoulder. "Claire? What happened to you?"

"Oh my god," Hazel said. She wrapped her arm around me and gave me a squeeze. "I was so scared!"

I stared into Sara's eyes and reached up to grab her arm. "I remember it all! What the woman said!"

She shook her head. "What? Slow down for a second! What woman?"

"The woman in the tower in the crystal city, the Menagerie's plan, Rennia... the end of the world! Right! That's happening! We have to change everything!"

"Crystal city? Claire, you're not making sense."

I insisted. "You know, the crystal city! Magical girls have to change the world today!"

Hazel looked to the rest of the band, searching for any shred of clarity. "What's she talking about?"

"Well," Nova said, "if we told ya that, Hazel babe, we'd be breakin' a real big rule."

"We *can't* tell you," Sara said.

I shook my head as I got back on my feet. "It doesn't matter anymore! Bloom's already pulled the curtain back. We have to go public to save the world! Everything's changing today, and we don't have a choice!"

"Save the *world?*" Hazel asked. "Claire, please tell me the truth, okay?"

Sara looked at me, sighed, and nodded. "Go ahead."

I turned to Hazel and took a deep breath. She was going to find out the truth about us—about *me*—one way or another. There was no way to avoid it now. That inevitability didn't make me less nervous. I had no clue how she'd react to this news. Her girlfriend being a supernatural magical being with powers beyond human understanding might be hard to swallow. At this point, there were no options left but to rip that bandage straight off.

I took her hand and looked into her eyes. "Haze, I don't know the best way to say this, so I guess I'll just say it. We're not just a band. We're... magical girls."

She flinched. "Magical girls? Like, from anime?"

"More or less."

"And that Bloom girl, the reason she looked like Iris—"

"Iris is a magical girl, too," Sara said, "and Bloom is a corrupted consciousness possessing her body."

"She's trying to bring about the end of the world," I added.

Nova laughed nervously and shrugged. "It's like that sometimes!"

"Okay, magical girls," Hazel said. Her eyes met mine and she blushed. "So, like ... do you get to wear cute outfits?"

"We do, yeah," I said. "Transformation sequence and everything."

Hazel grinned.

Cass looked at her curiously. "I gotta say, you're handling this a lot better than I expected."

"I already knew my girlfriend was magical," Hazel said. "So how are you gonna save the world?"

"I'm curious about that, too," Hana said. "Did you learn something from this woman in a crystal city?"

I nodded. "She said that when I transform, this magica in me is going to tell the Maidensong to unlock our true powers."

"True powers? What the flam's that mean?" Nova asked.

"I don't know, exactly. I just know we're in big trouble if Rennia—"

A low, booming, droning sound blasted across the city like a cosmic groan of anguish. It came from all sides, inescapable and oppressive. People in the market grabbed the sides of their heads as the sound smothered them.

"What is that?" Hazel asked, clutching her ears.

Our wrist links buzzed the "urgent" pattern, and the commander's voice crackled out, a mess of digital noise and dropouts.

"What... stat... or grid is... owing up. Tokyo HQ is... omms... alling an emerg... secrecy prot... uspended. Callin... backup... de Everg... e Ros... hold the r... f the city, but..."

Sara tapped and tried to respond. "Commander? Did not copy, say again! Commander?"

The call became even more distorted and unintelligible before finally cutting off for good. Our links' screens switched to the city's sensor grid and flashed a warning in red block lettering: UN-KNOWN INCURSION EVENT.

A series of loud bangs exploded along the riverfront as dozens of crackling, turbulent masses of energy burst into existence out of thin air. They elongated into rippling human-sized oblong forms, flat and vertical like doors, ragged red edges sinking into black voids beyond. From those voids, the familiar iridescent chitin of Pandora Corruption creatures began pushing their way out, disgorging from whatever alien dimension they came from. They truly were doors, portals from somewhere distant and nightmarish.

The invasion of Portland had begun.

| 16 |

Pandora Corruption creatures poured out of the portals along the river and began advancing, throwing the Saturday Market into total chaos. People screamed and ran, desperate to get away, knocking into each other and toppling tables and displays as a pack of creatures started to chase them.

The situation had escalated, and it was already spiraling out of control.

"Nope, no way! Not happening, creepos!" Nova shouted. She picked up a metal folding chair from an empty artist's tent and hurled it at the closest creature of the group. It sailed through the air and smacked into the monster's face, and the pack stopped, turned in our direction, and began to close the distance.

One of the creatures lunged for a food cart, abandoned by its owner as they fled the scene. It jammed its spike arms into the cart, and with a guttural roar, heaved it into the air toward us. I grabbed Hazel as the six of us dodged to the side. The cart smashed into the pavement, leaving behind a crumpled mess of debris.

Cass glared at the approaching creatures as we stood like a shield in front of Hazel. "Alright, I think we've got their attention. What's the plan, boss?"

Sara turned to me. "Claire, are you ready to do whatever it is you're supposed to do?"

I gulped. "Ready as I'll ever be. I don't actually know what's going to happen, though."

"Let us worry about that. Do it."

"Okay," I said. I looked back at Hazel, grabbed her hand, and gave it a squeeze. "Haze, you're about to see some, uh, stuff."

"What kind of stuff?" Hazel asked.

"This!"

I raised my hand up and my microphone materialized into my grip. As it surged with magica, I lowered it to my lips—and everything began to move slowly. Just as it had on the night of my awakening, time was grinding to a near-stop.

And then, I heard the voice of the Maidensong again.

You have learned the seriousness of the situation.

I nodded. "Yeah, I have. And I know about our true power."

Then the day of rebirth has arrived.

"That's what the lady in the crystal city told me, yeah."

I sense her magica in you, yes. You carry Adia's calling card.

The name was new to me, but it felt familiar. Comforting, even.

"She told me we'd change the world. I'm just not sure how to do that."

You have already proven yourself. You and your sisters will do great things.

Somewhere inside of me, just as I had on the night of my awakening, I felt the thrill, the sensation of confidence and ability and power. The knowledge that I could do this.

I was a girl. And I was a hero.

"I'm ready. What do you need me to do?"

All you must do is open your heart, and go forth with pride, my maiden.

For the span of a heartbeat, the world hung in silence, waiting for me to take the next step. And as time snapped back to normal, I took that step and cried out with all my heart into the microphone.

"Maidensong harmony power ... GO LIVE!"

In a microsecond, everything changed.

A whirlwind of rainbow-hued energy engulfed us. I felt the very fabric of creation itself being rattled and warped by the unimaginable power that surged from beyond our dimension through every cell in my body. Time and space opened up before me, and I saw every magical girl on Earth simultaneously, each stunned as the unbridled power of the Maidensong wailed and reverberated across the planet in a soaring chorus of impossible notes and harmonies.

My body glowed with a brilliant light of magica that far surpassed any previous transformation, and for a fleeting moment, my consciousness expanded to encompass *everything*, all dimensions once joined and now separate, every divergent world line that spiraled out through possibility and inevitability in trillions of combinations.

It was overwhelming and exhilarating and achingly beautiful and humbling, and in another instant, it faded from view.

With a jolt of raw magic power, Sara, Cass, Hana, Nova, and I shot into the sky like radiant chromatic missiles, soaring away from Portland. We blazed ever brighter with a kaleidoscope of hues as the world fell away beneath us.

We burst into an inky black expanse sparkling with starlight and shimmering crystalline glyphs, knowledge beyond my understanding, but which seemed familiar all the same. Below us, iridescent clouds swirled and undulated in complex patterns around the shaft of rainbow light that brought us here. I could not decide if we were floating among the stars above the planet, or in some impossible dimension far beyond reality as we understood it.

A massive geometric magica disc, a far grander version of the one that had ferried me up the tower, materialized beneath our feet. Overhead, a vast and soaring latticework dome of crystal appeared and gleamed with energy. It began to dawn on me that this was a place that magical girls of old must have known, and at that realization, the phrase "celestial stage" came back to me from some long-ago memory buried in my subconscious.

Swirling rivers of rainbow energy surged through the crystal dome and down into our bodies. This transformation would be done as a group, our hearts unified by the radiant connection between us as magical girls.

In that moment, I felt Sara's hand grasp mine. At the limit of my vision, she also took Cass's, who held Hana's, who held Nova's, who completed the circle with my other hand. Together, we drank in the life-affirming magica of the song, and of the lineage of girls who came before us, as an incredible soft warmth wrapped us up and cradled us.

I had never felt anything even remotely like this in my time in Magica Riot, or in my entire life. And in that moment, as the energy of all those connections—across dimensions, across world lines, backward and forward and sideways through time itself—flowed through me, I realized that *nobody* had felt like this for hundreds, or possibly thousands, of years. Not since Adia's time.

The glowing energy exploded off us, carrying our street clothes with it in hundreds of shards that dissipated into the aether. The purple river of magica embracing me began to snake around my body like living ribbons, clinging to me as it morphed into the pieces of my costume.

No, not the same costume. It was similar, but subtly different. My jacket had a different cut and a new overall purple hue, with studded lapels. Around my neck, a purple bow formed, with asymmetric ribbons hanging down my chest. My skirt flowed and angled more dramatically from its short front to its long back, the hem ringed in purple that matched a shimmering lining.

I wasn't alone in my new look. Sara wore a formal collared red-hued jacket with a matching bow, looking downright princely. Cass's yellow-tinged jacket had a wraparound cut joined by a longer skirt. Hana gained a belt and green bow to go with her newly green-tinted jacket. And Nova now wore a miniskirt and thigh highs along with a blue bow and an unbuttoned blue-hued jacket.

We still very much looked like a team, but now each had an individuality to our costumes. This was more than just a new outward appearance; along with unlocking our true power, we were unlocking our true *selves* as unique magical girls.

While our costumes formed, the colors of our hair transformed to match them. Sara's natural red grew bold and vibrant. Cass's twist-out had golden highlights woven throughout her locks. Hana's long dark brown ponytail now glowed a stunning emerald green. Nova's dyed pink twintails shifted completely into a bold, vivid blue. And, as my own hair swirled around me, my natural brown suddenly became a striking purple.

I felt the energy of the transformation reaching a new peak, stronger than I'd ever known before. The sensations were so tremendous and affirming that my eyes closed, this final surge sending me into a kind of magical euphoria. When my eyes opened again, I gazed into the faces of the other girls, and gasped; our eyes gleamed in bright hues matching our colors.

It was then that the voice of the Maidensong rang out across space and filled the crystalline dome.

THOSE EXALTED BY THE MAIDENSONG SHALL WIELD THE POWER OF HARMONY. AS IT WAS, SO IT SHALL BE.

Just as quickly as it had appeared, the crystal dome faded from view as the rainbow light returned and formed a sphere around us. We descended, crossing whatever distance we'd been from Portland in the blink of an eye. The rainbow orb carrying us smashed back into the pavement and blasted its colors out across the park when we landed.

As the rainbow glow subsided, my body felt fully alive, every cell buzzing with magica, saturated with newfound power. My skin tingled with joy and anticipation as I breathed deeply, savoring the sensation of raw, total life, as if my senses were heightened to thousands of times their normal capacity.

Sara spoke first as she took a confident step toward the Pandora Corruption creatures. "We are the guardians of song and heart. Guardian of Lyricism, Riot Red!"

Cass joined her, standing defiantly with her hands on her hips. "Guardian of Melody, Riot Yellow!"

Hana stepped forward, shoulder-to-shoulder with Cass, and shouted down the Pandora horde. "Guardian of Rhythm, Riot Green!"

Nova took a step and shot a grin toward the massing monsters. "Guardian of the Beat, Riot Blue!"

I moved forward, raised my arm, and pointed at the Pandora creatures, staring them down as the final words of transformation passed my lips. "Guardian of Harmony, Riot Purple! Servants of the darkness, be silenced by the song of Magica Riot!"

From behind me, I heard a soft gasp and looked back; Hazel was staring at me, her jaw hanging open.

"Claire?!"

My confidence burning inside me like a bonfire, I winked and nodded at her. "Hey, Haze."

A grin crossed her face and she let out an adorable half-laugh. "Um, that ... *wow*."

Hazel wasn't the only one staring. Predictably, five ordinary girls transforming into magical beings in a flash of rainbows had caused a bit of a stir, and those who weren't running for their lives had pulled out their phones to capture the moment.

Sara turned toward the crowd and addressed them with her arms raised. "People of Portland, please stay back! Clear the area and get to safety! These creatures are extremely dangerous! You can't fight them!"

As if to drive the point home, the Pandora creatures shrieked and charged toward us, their shells clacking, arm spikes raised at the ready. Behind them, more stepped out of the portals, quickly getting a bead on us.

Sara turned her attention back to them. "Let's go to work."

My keytar materialized, its strap falling around my neck and shoulders. It glowed and thrummed; even now, I could feel the incredible power coursing through it, surging past the old wall that had marked the upper limit of our abilities.

"Stay back, Haze," I said, looking back over my shoulder. "We'll handle this."

Hazel didn't answer, but her dreamy-eyed stare spoke volumes.

Sara played the opening chords of "Second Promise, Second Chance" and we braced ourselves for combat. The oncoming, snarling horde of Pandora creatures closed in, spiked arms raised to strike. I tensed my legs, played a riff on my keytar, and leapt at them as they came within attack distance.

One of the creatures swung at me, trying to skewer me. I pushed off to the side and dove beneath its arm. It missed me by inches, and I spun around to slam the keytar into its body. My attack landed square and true, and the head of the keytar smashed into the creature's shell with a loud, wet *crack*. Viscous fluid streaked with black goo dribbled out of the wound as the creature screamed. With a final jab, I fired a bolt of magica into it at point-blank range.

I had prepared to dodge around and come in for another attack, but my magica blasted straight through the creature's body and out the other side, raining wet, otherworldly chunks onto the pavement. A moment later, the creature dropped lifelessly to the pavement and began to dissolve.

My eyes met Sara's as she stood over another creature's dissolving corpse and a mist of pulverized shell and goop, her guitar axe having sliced its head off with a single stroke. We exchanged silent looks of surprise before turning and attacking the next wave of creatures. These, too, fell to our instruments, as did the third wave.

"Don't these jerks usually put up more of a fight?" Nova asked.

"They've never gone up against fully powered magical girls before," Hana said.

Cass blasted another creature as it stepped out of a portal. "If they weren't throwing so many of them at us, we'd have this in the bag already."

Sara swung her guitar at another arriving creature and sliced its head off as it stepped through the portal. "If we stick to the portals here and figure out how to close them, we can stop this before it—"

A round of screams from farther down the riverfront interrupted us. There, dozens more portals ripped open, one by one, in quick succession.

"Crap," Sara said. "Okay, new plan! Blue and I will stay here and hold this part of the park. Yellow, Purple, Green, head down and deal with the new portals. Let's hold the line until we can figure out how to close them!"

"You've got it, Red," Cass said.

I ran back over to Hazel and took her hand. "Haze, you've got to get out of here. This is really dangerous, and we don't know what's going to happen."

"No argument here," she said. "Hey, you know what? I was right."

"About what?"

"You do look great with purple hair." She leaned into me and kissed me, lingering softly for a long moment before pulling back. "Come back safe."

"I will, I promise."

She smiled. "Alright. Go save the world, rock star."

| 17 |

I watched as Hazel escaped into the city before I returned to Cass and Hana. The three of us took off running in the direction of the new set of portals; the first batch of Pandora creatures that stepped out of them were now chasing people in the crowd, and it would be safest to find a way to separate them.

"Let's break this up," I said. "Green, can you give us a wall?"

Hana plucked and slapped at her bass as she zeroed in on the creatures in front. "Get ready! Setting them up ..."

Her fingers flew over the strings of her fretboard, channeling a bolt of magica that erupted from the ground with a loud, percussive *thwack*. A giant wall of green energy snaked its way in front of the Pandora creatures, slamming into them as they pursued their human targets. The creatures were left stunned and disoriented, stumbling back from the barrier as they tried to regroup.

Cass and I took aim, locked into a synchronized riff, and charged up our own shots.

"... and knocking them down!" Cass shouted as we fired. Our magica sliced through the creatures' shells, ripping them open and spilling the mess inside across the grass.

The next waves of creatures had shifted course, ignoring the innocents and coming at us instead. I nudged Hana's shoulder and played a chord to recharge my magica. "Give me the rhythm and I'll hit them with the lead!"

Hana grinned back at me. "With pleasure!"

I ran for the creatures as she thumped out another driving bass line. Shockwaves of green magica pulsed into them, knocking them off-balance and opening up a perfect opportunity to hit them hard.

I dove in, thrusting and slicing my keytar as I wove my way through the horde. Purple streaks of energy arced through the air as I smashed into the first target, cracking apart its shell and sending it toppling to the ground. I pushed through, hitting a second and a third and a fourth while Cass sniped the others from a distance.

"These creeps are gonna have to do better than this," Cass said. "This is just target practice!"

"Wait," Hana said. "I feel something."

I felled the last of the wave and ran back to her side. "What kind of something?"

She placed a hand on the side of her head. "Hard to explain. I just feel something coming."

I aimed my keytar at the row of portals, expecting another wave, which is when several new, *larger* portals ripped open behind the first set.

Hulking new figures pushed their way out. Like the Pandora creatures we knew, they were made of that shimmering, iridescent chitin, but they towered twenty feet above us. Their eyes blazed a fiery red, looking down at us not with the blank vacancy of the normal creatures, but with raw malice. They each had four huge spiked arms, and their bulk glistened and dripped with fluid, as though they had been birthed from some cosmic orifice. Rivulets of red and black dripped from mouths that looked purpose-built to gnash and devour.

"There they are," Hana said.

"What are they?" Cass asked.

I felt an ancient, long-buried recognition flow through me from the Maidensong. "I think that's what the Pandora Corruption used to be."

Cass aimed her guitar at the giants. "If they're Pandoras, they can be killed, no matter how big and nasty they are!"

She fired bolts of magica at them, which slammed into their shells and glanced off.

"That didn't even make them flinch," Hana said.

Cass looked to me and I aimed my keytar. We both tried again, firing simultaneously, but got the same result. The giants kept advancing, slowly but steadily.

"Thoughts?" I asked.

Cass frowned. "Let's try something different!"

"What do you have in mind?"

"I'll draw their attention, and you two get in there and hit 'em up close. Green, you boost, and Purple, you smash. Sound good?"

"It's worth a try," Hana said. "We can't let those things get into the city!"

I nodded. "Ready!"

We ran straight for the giants, focusing on the closest. Hana's fingers leapt and slid across her bass strings, and my keytar came to life. Magica flowed between us like a river. The keytar tingled and thrummed beneath my fingertips, finally free of the limits it used to fight against, and my body responded in kind. Life and power surged through me as we rushed the giants.

The creature glared down at us, just as huge bolts of Cass's yellow magica punched it in the face. It roared, spewing wet strings of its putrid bile through the air, and looked up in her direction.

"There's our opening!" Hana shouted.

"On it!" I yelled back.

I pushed off the ground, hurling myself straight at the giant's torso, and pulled back my keytar to strike. My magica resonated with Hana's, and my muscles burned as I swung at the monster's center of mass. Where I had once felt "the wall" restraining my attack, now I only felt power.

As I brought the keytar down onto the giant's shell, a shimmering purple blade of magica materialized, an extension of the instrument's body. That blade sliced into the giant's chitin, ripping a gash into its shell.

I thrust down through the monster's body and kicked off, backflipping away as slime oozed from the gash. The giant staggered back, roaring and gurgling as it struggled to stay up, the glow in its eyes dimming.

"We can do it!" I shouted. "We can take them ou—"

I froze as two of the giant's companions jabbed its back with their spiked arms. The injured creature's shell glowed with radiant energy. At its wound, the shell liquified, and re-flowed to seal up the gash. The hateful fire of its eyes returned.

"Oh *come on!*"

Cass ran up and glared at the giants. "They are not getting off that easy. It's time to take these things down! Clear out, I'm doing this!"

"*What* are you doing?" Hana asked.

"Improvising! I'm taking the solo!"

Suddenly, her body glowed with radiant yellow magica and she began to levitate.

I stared up at her as she floated higher and higher. "How are you doing that?!"

"Not sure! Just get back!"

Hana and I ran away from the giants as Cass rose up above them. Streams of magica swirled around her as she raised her hand. Her microphone materialized into it, and she lowered it to her mouth as she pointed at the creatures with her other hand.

"Maidensong Melody Severance!"

Moving as if guided by the Maidensong itself, Cass's hands flew across her guitar's fretboard in a vicious guitar solo. Crackling yellow magica arced around her like the hands of a clock. At the end of those hands, eight glowing duplicates of her guitar materialized in a ring from her head to her feet, aimed down at the giants below her.

Cass played on, louder, more ferociously, and those guitars fired.

Eye-searing blasts of magica ripped out of the guitars in rapid succession and drilled into the giants, eviscerating their shells everywhere they impacted. The assault was relentless. The giants screamed as their bodies disintegrated around them.

Within seconds, it was over.

What was left of the giants fell limp and ragged to the ground. The glowing guitars around Cass disappeared, and she floated back down. Her feet touched the grass and she stumbled to her knees, panting and sweating.

"Are you okay?" I asked.

"Yeah, yeah, I'm fine. That just—wow, it takes a lot out of you."

Hana kneeled beside her and squeezed her shoulder. "Just take it easy. What exactly *was* that?"

"Don't know. Got this vision, I guess. Like I remembered something I forgot."

"I think you did," I said. "Adia told me our true powers would come back to us. I guess this is what she meant."

The sounds of fighting and screaming drew our attention back toward the Saturday Market. A group of giants had appeared there, too, smashing their way toward the core of the city.

Cass got back on her feet. "Let's go help Red and Blue. We know how to kill these things now."

We found Sara and Nova surrounded, fending off a trio of Pandora giants. They had taken cover under the metal and glass awnings of the market, but the creatures were relentless. With sheer brute strength, the giants smashed through the awnings and slammed their spike arms down in an attempt to reach them.

Hana summoned a wall of magica as all three of us dove for cover beside them.

"Status, boss?" Cass asked.

"Not great," Sara said. "We can't do enough damage to these things."

"Gettin' real tired of these creepos smashin' up our city," Nova said.

"I think we figured out a way to deal with that," I said.

"Yes," Hana nodded. "The very short version is: we have special attacks now!"

"Special attacks?" Sara asked. "What are you talking about?"

"Focus," Cass said. "Concentrate on the Maidensong. It'll come to you. Worked for me!"

Sara took a deep breath. "Alright. Cover me!"

She ran out into the open and stared down the approaching giants. The creatures stomped toward her, cracking and shaking the pavement with each step.

Sara's fists clenched as the closest giant pulled back one of its arms to strike—and then, she relaxed.

"I think—yeah, I've got it! Riot Chorus Sonic Blade!"

She played an overdriven chord progression as she sung out an angry, primal melody that pierced the air. Sharp-edged rings of red magica swirled around the giants, trapping them in a nightmare of glowing blades. Enraged, the creatures thrashed and pounded against the rings, but they held, pulsing with Sara's furious performance.

More rings appeared, interlocking and overlapping until they completely enclosed the giants. With a final, heart-rending chord, Sara's guitar and vocals blasted out a deafening roar. The rings glowed and constricted, slicing through the monsters' shells like a knife through silk.

The giants screamed for only a moment before they were silenced, their massive bodies collapsing into piles of chitinous strips.

Sara fell to the ground, panting. "You weren't kidding, Yellow."

"Just take it easy," Cass said. "Catch your breath."

"There's still creatures coming out of the portals," I said. "Probably more giants coming. How is all this supposed to bring Rennia back?"

"For real, it's just chaos so far."

"Chaos," Hana repeated as she furrowed her brow and shook her head. "How does it all connect ..." She paused; she looked like she was trying to make out a conversation at the edge of hearing. "Oh no. Oh no. There's something else—"

The earth itself began to shake as a distant, muffled roar filled the air and echoed through downtown. Glass in the buildings across the street from the park shattered and rained down on the sidewalk.

"Don't tell me we've got a flammin' earthquake now," Nova said.

Hana looked up in the direction of the river, her eyes wide with shock. "It's not an earthquake. Chaos has come for us again."

I turned around, following Hana's gaze, just in time to see a burst of red magica explode beneath the water of the Willamette River. The water swelled up and exploded, blasting fifty feet into the air, and from within the spray emerged a massive iridescent insect leg.

It slammed into the pavement of the market plaza as water spilled out into the park. Another leg followed it, digging into the ground as the pair hauled something up from the river.

Slowly, an enormous beetle-like creature the size of a cargo ship rose from the water. Its slimy iridescent shell was like those of the other Pandora creatures, on a far larger scale and supported by six of those huge legs. Its head was covered in angry, glowing red eyes. Below them, spiked pincers framed an oozing maw of tendrils, and from the top of its head jutted a crystalline horn of corrupted red thaumatite.

"Oh, that's *big* big," Cass murmured.

Nova jumped back and pointed up at the creature. "What the fuck is that thing?!"

"I thought heroes don't curse!" I said.

"Babe, I ain't feeling heroic right this second!"

Above us, the monster dipped its head down, aiming its thaumatite horn directly at us.

"Um, if that's thaumatite, does that mean what I think it means?" Hana asked.

Leaving no doubt, the horn glowed vibrant crimson as the creature let out a wet, guttural roar.

"We need to move," Sara said. "Right now!"

A beam of magica shot out of the horn, ripping apart the pavement. We leapt out of the way as it gouged a deep wound in the earth below and sliced all the way through the park into Naito Parkway, the road that ran alongside the river. Pulverized concrete dust blew across the park as we got back on our feet.

"Do we have a plan for this?" I asked.

Sara shook her head. "Never fought anything this big before. We're a little off-book!"

The creature's horn glowed again, and it fired another blast across the park. The beam sliced into a building across the street and blasted out the back, instantly wrecking the integrity of its walls and triggering a collapse. Concrete and brick exploded away from the building, raining down on the street below as it fell.

Impossibly, the monster advanced. The ground in the path of its beam lay cooked and steaming. It followed this path like a roadway, its colossal footsteps smacking the ground with each step.

It was now heading into the heart of the city.

"That thing's gonna take out half of downtown," Nova said. "We gotta do something!"

"Can we even hurt something like that?" Hana asked.

Cass called down her guitar again and aimed at the creature's underbelly as it passed overhead. "Only one way to find out!"

She played a snarling, overcharged riff and fired a blast up into the creature's shell. The shot exploded square and true, strong enough to blast a hole through any conventional Pandora Corruption monster. With *this* monster, it dissipated harmlessly against its chitin, leaving not even so much as a blast mark.

Hana shook her head. "Something this large is probably more magica than matter. It has to be nearly impervious."

Nova's face lit up. "That just means we gotta hit it *harder*, babes!"

"I'm still recovering from my first special move," Cass said. "I don't think I have it in me right now to—"

"Naw, naw, I got ya," Nova grinned. "Watch me work!" She ran out into the ruined plaza behind the bug as it pushed its way into the city.

Sara reached for her as she dashed off. "Blue! What are you doing?"

"I dunno, it just came to me!"

Nova raised her hands up as her drum sticks materialized in her grasp and her drum kit appeared before her. With a look of determination, she lowered the right stick and pointed directly at the monster as she started to play.

"Beat Stream Blizzard!"

Dozens of her glowing blue holo-drums—no, *hundreds* of them—appeared above the monster, like a self-contained thundercloud. Shockwaves of blue magica rained down from the cloud with every beat she played, smashing into the bug from multiple angles at once.

The pummeling was relentless, and the creature bucked and roared in fury, shaking the ground as it raged. Keeping the beat, Nova doubled her tempo, rolling into a massive drum fill as she glowed with energy, pummeling the monster with hit after hit. So many that, for a few moments, it was hard to even make out its shape.

Her drum solo reached its apex—a single, dramatic crash. The entire cloud of drums blasted the creature at once, kicking up a cloud of dust. Nova fell to a knee, her face glistening with sweat as she laughed.

"Down you go, big guy!"

A scream like thunder blasted across the city. The bug emerged from the dust cloud, enraged and moving faster as it pushed its way farther into downtown. Its shell scraped against buildings as it went, sending glass and concrete and stone falling to the pavement.

"That's no fair!" Nova shouted.

"All we've done is make it angry," Sara said. "We need a real plan!"

"How are we going to stop something like that?" I asked.

"Boss, what about the Menagerie?" Cass asked. "Rennia? We don't even know how they're freeing her, or where, or—"

"Everybody STOP!"

Hana raised a finger, calling for quiet, as she laid her other hand to the side of her head. Her expression was serious, focused. She looked like she was trying to pick out a distant song, faintly audible on the breeze, but...

"What is it, babe?" Nova asked.

Hana looked up and smiled. "I feel it."

Cass stared at her in confusion. "You feel *what?*"

"The rhythm. The Maidensong is a manifestation of magica. Magica has a rhythm. Corrupted magica has a rhythm. When that monster screamed just now, it hit me—I feel it!"

Sara stepped closer to her. "Is this related to our new powers? You called yourself the Guardian of Rhythm when you transformed."

"I think so, yes. I'm starting to get it, how this all works." She stared ahead, feeling something none of us could sense. Then, she beamed. "I think I know what the Menagerie is doing!"

"Lay it out," Cass said, "but quickly."

Hana paced back and forth as she spoke. "Our magica, the Maidensong, thrives on harmony. The corrupted magica of the Pandora beings thrives on chaos. The Menagerie is ripping open the fabric and letting all these Pandora monsters come over because every one of them adds chaos to the world. When they attack innocents, when they fight us, when bigger and meaner ones show up—chaos energy!"

"So are we just supposed to not fight 'em?" Nova asked.

Hana shook her head. "No, it's going to happen whether we're here or not. If we fight or don't, the creatures attack either way. They're collecting all this energy and pumping it back through the Alliance's sensor network!"

"That's why they stole the data on it," I said.

"Exactly! They're using the network like—like a giant amplifier! And feeding the signal into one spot!"

"What spot?" Sara asked.

Hana closed her eyes for a moment, then spun around and pointed. "There!"

We followed her gaze to the partially constructed skyscraper at the corner of Alder and Tenth, the Chamber of Commerce's new favorite toy: the Grand Sovereign Hotel.

It was one of the tallest things in the city, and it was currently unoccupied. A perfect thing to use as a giant magica receiver.

"That's where the gate to Rennia is," Cass said. "It's got to be. We have our target."

"What about the dang bug stompin' around?" Nova asked. "It's gonna hurt people! We can't just let it go free!"

Cass shook her head. "We just saw it shrug off your big special attack. Besides, how many people are going to be hurt when some evil corrupted goddess woman shows up and breaks the fabric of reality?"

"From what Green just said, we might not be able to stop 'em if that monster's alive!" Nova protested. "It's feedin' power into the system!"

Hana turned back to Sara. "What's your call, Red?"

Sara frowned and looked back and forth between the bug and the Grand Sovereign. "I—I don't know. We can only do one thing right now, and if we're wrong, a whole lot of people are going to suffer."

I gazed up toward the tower. Something Hana said stuck in the back of my mind, and it itched.

And then, clarity crashed into me like a runaway train.

"We don't choose," I said. "We do both."

"You have an idea?" Sara asked.

"Maybe, yeah. Green, you just said that the Menagerie was using the sensor network and the gate like an amplifier."

Hana nodded. "That's right."

"And this whole thing is about pushing chaos energy into the gate?"

"Yeah..."

"What if we haul the bug up there with us, blast it all with everything we have, and get the thing to feed back its own chaos energy directly into the gate, all at once?"

Cass grinned. "We blow the amp."

I pointed at her. "Exactly! We're a rock band, right? We can blow an amp!"

Nova leaned in closer, looking baffled. "How the heck are we gonna throw an interdimensional space bug the size of a blimp into a gate on top of a skyscraper?"

"Bugs can climb. We just need to give it a boost. You can trampoline it up!"

She laughed. "I can't trampoline a giant bug!"

I reached out and put my hand on her shoulder. "You trampolined a van. You can trampoline a bug!"

"I'm not sure that follows, actually," Hana said.

Cass thought for a moment. "How are we going to get the bug to feed back into the gate? Our biggest moves don't even hurt it!"

"We bring the bug and the gate together," I said, "and then we use the Exalted Harmony."

Hana raised her hand. "Sorry, we use what?"

"The Exalted Harmony. I, um, don't know what it is, but Adia told me to use it if we ran into something too powerful to defeat. This has to be what she meant."

"Only problem is, that's a lot to take on faith," Cass said.

"It is, yeah. I'm not sure what else to do."

Sara smiled. "I like it."

I blinked. "Uh ... you do?"

She nodded. "Don't get me wrong, it's absurd, but I like it. You're really thinking for yourself. That's the kind of thing Iris was always good at, too."

I nearly felt like crying. "That means a lot to me."

"There's an unknown factor here," Hana said. "The Menagerie. I doubt they're just going to stand there and let us do this."

"Oh, they won't," Sara said. "Which is why we're going to split up. I'll distract them while the rest of you herd the bug."

Cass shook her head and put her hands up. "Red, that's signing a death wish. I'm not going to let you face them down by yourself."

My heart leapt in my chest; Sara wasn't the only one with a connection to Iris and Bloom. I took a deep breath, and stepped forward.

"I'm going with you," I said.

"The flam you are," Sara said. Behind her, Nova pumped her fist.

A list of justifications flooded my mind; that Iris had entrusted the meeting with Adia to me, that both Sara and I had luck getting through to Bloom together, that two girls against the world was just about doable with good luck, that none of us needed to face anything alone ever again.

Instead, I landed on the silliest reason of them all.

"What if you need another absurd plan?"

For a moment, I thought Sara was going to push back, but her expression softened. "Alright. Thank you."

"I can't believe we're doin' this," Nova said.

"We're not only doing it, we're going to make it work," Sara said. "You three go do whatever it takes to steer the bug over to the hotel and get it up on the roof. Purple and I will buy you time. No matter what, this ends here and now!"

| 18 |

Sara and I stared up at the top of of the Grand Sovereign from the sidewalk outside the construction entrance. Distant sounds of magica blasts and roars told us that Cass, Hana, and Nova had engaged the bug, and now, it was our turn.

"You want me to find the construction elevator?" I asked.

Sara closed her eyes for a moment, and smiled. "I'm remembering all these things magical girls used to know. We've got a shortcut."

Glowing, geometric sigils of spinning magica appeared beneath her feet. I recognized it as a variant of the spell that had carried me up the tower in the crystal city, and with a moment's thought, I created one beneath me as well.

Sara looked over at me. "How are you feeling? Ready to do this?"

I wasn't sure if I genuinely believed the words I next spoke, or if I was intoxicated by the true power of the Maidensong. The effect was the same, either way.

"Of course I'm ready. We're magical girls! This is what we do!"

She smiled and took my hand, giving it a tight squeeze. "Couldn't have said it better myself."

The sigils beneath our feet spun faster, glowing with intense magica. A heartbeat later, we blasted off, straight up into the sky.

The tower's half-complete exterior rushed past us as we soared up its side, crested the roof, and dropped back down for a landing.

A jagged arch made of corrupted thaumatite crystals and wiring stood in the center of the rooftop, glowing with the Pandora Corruption power that flowed from across the city. In the center of the arch, a pinprick of turbulent red energy roiled and crackled. If anything up here was the gate, this was certainly it.

Tending to the gate were the members of the Menagerie. Blaze and Burst stood together, on the far side of the arch from Sara and me. Bloom was closer, facing away from us, but she clearly sensed our arrival.

She turned around and shot us a smile of sinister intent. "Well, look at you! You got quite a glow-up! I almost didn't recognize you tw—wait, aren't you a little short-staffed?"

I saw a chance to feed Bloom's ego with deception. "We've suffered some unfortunate losses, which is why we're here to talk."

The other two noticed us and circled around the arch to join her.

"Amazing timing," Blaze said. "True magical girls have returned, just in time to get put in their place by Mistress Rennia. The Maidensong really is in decline."

"At least it's going to make this more fun," Burst laughed. "Never thought I'd get the chance to kill *real* magical girls."

Sara stepped forward and leveled her gaze at the Menagerie trio. "We can solve this peacefully. Nobody else has to get hurt."

"I'm sorry, do you think you have the upper hand here?" Bloom asked. "Look around you, Magica Riot! It's over! The dimension gate is on a build-up to opening. Rennia's army is walking the streets of the city. We've already won!"

"It's never too late to do the right thing," I said. "You're going to have a lot of pain and suffering on that conscience you're developing."

"Bloom, what is she talking about?" Burst asked.

"*Nothing*," Bloom spat. "And you, Claire. Shut up."

There it was: our opening. Sara and I exchanged looks; since we hadn't yet been interrupted by the bug, I could press harder. "You've changed, haven't you? Somewhere inside you, Iris taught you to feel bad about what you're doing."

Bloom glared at me. "Shut *up!* I don't feel bad about anything I've done."

"Keep telling yourself that," Sara said. "We know the truth. Iris is more powerful than you bargained for."

Burst and Blaze gave Bloom suspicious looks.

"This might explain why you've been so distracted lately," Burst said. "Like you haven't been fully committed to Mistress's vision."

"How *dare* you," Bloom snarled. "I was chosen to carry out Mistress's will, and I never leave a job half-finished, for—"

"For better or worse," Sara interrupted. "Just like Iris always said."

"You've had a taste of independence, and it's intoxicating, isn't it?" I smiled. "I know how it feels to find yourself after being lost for so long."

"Stop it!" Bloom shouted. "You don't know anything! Mistress has the power to reshape the world!"

I sighed and looked past her, out across the city to the distant peak of Mt. Hood, barely visible through the rain and clouds. "Listen to what you're saying. There are six hundred and fifty thousand people in this city. Billions on this planet. People going about their days, living their hopes and dreams. You'd hand those lives to a monster's lust for power and blood. That's despicable. Nobody carrying the heart of a maiden could live with themselves after that."

"I don't have the heart of a maiden!"

Sara moved up beside me and shook her head. "But you do. You can feel Iris's heart right now."

The other girls had still not yet arrived with the bug, so I continued to turn the screws on Bloom's willpower. "Magical girls can change the world for the better. I've seen how the world used to be. It can be like that again. Stop this and help us."

Sara took another step closer to Bloom. "I know who'd do the right thing. Iris—you can hear me in there, can't you?"

Bloom backed up as her face twitched, her mouth curling into a frown. "No! Get away from me!"

"What are you doing to her? Stop this immediately!" Blaze shouted.

Sara ignored her and pushed on. "Sweetheart, it's me. Claire, too. We're here to stop the gate. We need help to convince your new friend."

"Shut your mouth!" Bloom snapped.

"I know you can help us, Iris," Sara continued. "I love you *so* much. Reach out to me and help us save the world, okay?"

Bloom dropped to a knee and grabbed the sides of her head. She groaned, her face contorted and angry, as a telltale trickle of blood ran from her nose. "You're not doing this to me! You're not ... not going to make me ..."

Suddenly, a terrible gurgling moan escaped her mouth and she collapsed onto the rooftop, twitching and writhing around.

Burst glared at me. "Screw this. Let's just kill them!"

By the time I heard her words, she was already on me, swinging her glowing, magica-charged fist. I called down my keytar and ducked beneath, smashing the neck of the keytar into her stomach. The blast knocked her back just long enough to let me regroup.

Near the roof's edge, Sara rushed forward, smashing Blaze's shoulder with her guitar. With Bloom temporarily out of commission, the fight was even, but there was no telling how long that would last.

Burst ran at me again and threw another glowing fist at my face. I brought up my keytar and blocked it, straining as the muscles of my arms burned. She was even stronger than before, no doubt feeding off the tremendous amounts of corruption energy saturating the city.

"Stop this," I said, "or I'll make you stop!"

She grinned maliciously at me. "What are you gonna do, bite me again? Chaos has only made us stronger! We are unstoppable!"

"No, you're overconfident!" I focused on the Maidensong and swung at her. The purple magica blade materialized on my keytar again as I sliced up her chest and into her jaw.

She shoved me back, glaring at me with blood trickling down her cheek as a red disc of magica appeared behind her.

"I'm getting *very* tired of you making me bleed, Riot Purple! I think it's time I returned the favor!" She leapt up and planted her feet on the disc, and shouted "Midnight Sledge!"

With a flash of light, she launched off the disc and flew at me, an angry blast of energy rippling through the air ahead of her. I braced against the rooftop and held up my hands, forming my own magica sigil in front of me.

Burst slammed into it at top speed as her attack exploded. I shoved back, my sigil spinning, the geometric patterns a blur. Our magica locked in a vicious whirlwind, each spell counteracting the other.

"You cannot stop Rennia!" Burst shouted through the storm of energy. "Power and strength always triumph in the end!"

A gale of magica whipped around me. I staggered and shoved back against her. "You're wrong, Burst! Strength comes from kindness!"

"Let's see if you still think that as I rip you to pieces! You will—"

Then, without warning, she faltered. Her face wrenched with pain, and she screamed, raw and agonized. I had no idea what happened, but her momentary lapse of concentration was enough. I hurled myself forward, my sigil exploding against her magica, and she flew back, smashing into the rooftop and skidding away.

I was baffled. Sara was still busy with Blaze; she hadn't come to my rescue, so what had happened to hurt Burst like that?

And that's when I saw her: Bloom, her own blood smeared down her face and chest, holding Iris's keytar as it glowed with violet energy, still crackling after being fired.

She gestured in Burst's direction. "Finish the job already, Claire!"

I nodded, took a deep breath, and focused. A phrase appeared in my mind, carried on the sound of the Maidensong, and I knew exactly what I needed to do.

"Heart Synth Sonic Blossom!"

I played a complex chord as I levitated from the rooftop. The keytar glowed, resonating with hyper-charged magica. Five shimmering floral petals of purple and pink energy unfurled and grew from my body, framing me in the center of a glistening magical rose.

A huge, swirling blast leapt out from the petals. The shot slammed into Burst and blew her across the rooftop, leaving her crumpled in a heap against a piece of ventilation machinery.

Exhausted, I landed back on the roof and fell to my knees. As my body trembled and my lungs clawed for oxygen, I felt the calming steadiness of Sara's hand on my shoulder.

Blaze rushed to her fallen comrade's side while screaming daggers at Bloom.

"Betrayer! What have you done?!"

Bloom looked at her partners, shook her head, and walked over to join Sara and I. "Oh, hell. What's the fun in ruling a ruined world? That's hardly satisfying! Why should I play second fiddle to Rennia when I could be my own boss?" She glanced at Sara, and for a brief moment, I thought I saw a hint of softness in her expression. "Besides, this conscience is a pain, but it's not *wrong*. Maybe I don't want to be a damn monster."

"You think double-crossing Mistress Rennia will do anything for you?" Burst asked as she struggled to sit up with Blaze's help. "The gate's still going to open. She will rend your flesh from its bones as she will the rest of these pathetic people!"

And then, from somewhere hundreds of feet below us, I felt the tower trembling.

I stood back up. "About that—I think you're going to be surprised."

The trembling grew more noticeable.

"What are you babbling about now?" Blaze asked.

"Vile magical girls!" Burst shouted. "What did you do?!"

"You wanted chaos," I said. "We're giving you chaos!"

Sara chuckled at them. "You bought our lie about losing our team way too easily."

Bloom leaned in close to my ear. "No, seriously, Claire. What did you do?"

The entire skyscraper was now shaking under the force of what was, no doubt, scurrying its way up the side.

I stepped forward and smiled at Blaze and Burst. "You had everything perfectly planned out. Well, allow us to introduce a *bug* into things!"

The building kept shaking, but nothing else happened. I cleared my throat, and repeated myself.

"Allow us to introduce a *bug* into things!"

More shaking. I was starting to think I had underestimated how long it would take a blimp-sized bug to climb a skyscraper.

"Claire," Sara said, "you ... you really don't have to—"

"*Allow* us," I interrupted, "to *introduce*... a *bug*... into *th*—"

With a tremendous, world-shaking roar, the bug leapt up over the edge of the tower. Its six massive legs smashed down onto the roof as the skyscraper groaned under its weight. There was nowhere for it to go now. It thrashed around, its mouth pincers smashing against utility equipment and pipes, scattering them across the roof in twisted heaps.

The monster seemed to know it had no means of escape that didn't involve leaping to the street four hundred and fifty feet below. It bellowed again and blasted an angry beam from its horn that swept out across the city, vaporizing streaks into the overcast sky.

Time was critical now, before the bug destroyed the entire building. But it was *here*, and that gave us a fighting chance.

As the monster ransacked the rooftop, Blaze pulled Burst to her feet. They ran to the edge of the roof, and Burst shot me a look of seething anger.

"Don't think this means you've won, Magica Riot! You're already dead. The gate cannot be stopped!"

She and Blaze conjured discs of magica beneath their feet, and with a flash of energy, blasted themselves out into open air, shooting across the city.

Cass, Hana, and Nova sailed up and over the edge and landed on the roof in front of us. They were streaked with blood, black goop, and dust and debris, but appeared otherwise intact.

"One bug," Cass said.

"Signed, sealed, and delivered," Hana grinned.

Nova shook her head. "I NEVER WANT TO TALK ABOUT THIS EVER AGAIN ... oh, hi, Bloom!"

Bloom gasped. "How did you *do* this?!"

"We're saving the world," Cass said. "Join in, or get out of the way."

Bloom rolled her eyes. "Ugh. Nobody is going to take you girls seriously. You're too corny."

Sara reached over and grabbed my arm. "Claire, whatever this Exalted Harmony is, you need to use it *right now*. You're the Guardian of Harmony."

"Right," I said. "Exalted Harmony time. Everybody, get to the gate!"

The five of us dodged around the bug's stomping legs and sprinted to the gate, gathering in a circle around it. The red energy at its center glowed larger, more turbulent, and angrier as it grew, slowly but inexorably, toward opening.

Bloom stood nearby, using her red magica discs as shields. As she deflected the bug's flailing appendages, she looked back at me over her shoulder.

"Don't make me put up with this crap any longer than I have to, Claire! Whatever you're going to do, *do it!*"

I closed my eyes and focused on the words Adia had told me.

Exalted Harmony...

Energy struck me like a hammer to a bell. My ears rang with wordless harmonies reverberating across time and dimensions, loud enough to envelop the world itself. I could almost see it, the weave of the harmony, resonating and breathing life into the Maidensong.

I awakened to a cosmic truth. The Exalted Harmony was the collective voice of all magical girls, past, present, and future. Our shared heart, beating as one. The mighty raw river of magica that we shaped and channeled as magical girls.

Every cell of my body resonated with power, but I felt simultaneously at peace. I knew at that instant that no magical girl had experienced this for a very, very long time. This sensation had been locked away from us for generations as we worked with our senses dulled and our abilities restrained, living in darkness.

Today, Magica Riot was guiding magical girls everywhere back into the light.

I understood now that every magical girl's expression of the Exalted Harmony was unique, just as we were. The name and form of Magica Riot's Exalted Harmony entered my mind, and through our magica, I shared it with the other girls. In unison, we spoke the name of our Exalted Harmony.

"Riot Harmony Chordal Cataclysm!"

Five glowing strands of color pulled from each of us like yarn and braided loosely around each other. The strands formed a ring that encircled the bug monster and lifted it as if it were weightless; in perfect sync with the Exalted Harmony's driving beat, it glowed and pulsed with energy.

The music swelled, and I felt the weight of my keytar as it materialized in my hands. Nova counted us in, her drumsticks clacking to the rhythm. On the downbeat, we captured the song and took it over, shaping it into our own. As my hands flew between chords, I realized I'd always known how to play it; it felt like a song I'd loved in another time, another place, finally come back to me at last.

Above us, the bug—completely ensnared by the ever-constricting braid of magica—floated down toward the gate, which seemed somehow unnerved by its presence. The gate strained at its crystalline arch, as if trying to recoil in fear.

With her defensive job complete, Bloom took cover from the floating megaton-grade thaumatite bomb poised like a guillotine above the gate.

I heard Sara's voice first, singing a wordless vocalization, feeling out a new melody among the chords and tones. Cass joined her, then Nova, their voices lilting and sparkling in harmony.

A twinge spiked me deep inside. Would I have to sing?

Claire...

The new voice belonged to Adia, whispering and soft in my mind.

"No—I can't sing," I pleaded.

Her voice shone with gentle encouragement.

The final note must be delivered, my maiden.

Tears welled in my eyes. "Please don't make me sing."

Hana's voice joined the exalted chorus. Adia gently urged me.

This is the moment.

I can't. Don't make me sing. I can't do it. Not now, not ever.

Deliver the final note, Claire.

How could she sound so sure, so confident?

Begin the second age of magical girls.

I sobbed and squeezed my eyes shut, tight, straining. And...

There was red. The color, the idea, the emotion of anger and blood and war and violence stabbed at me from deep within the gate. I winced in pain, my skin searing and burning through my costume as the red sliced at my body.

Wailing, discordant harmonies of raw chaos poured out, razor-sharp shards of red like corrupted crystal wailing on the sound waves ripping out of the heart of the gate. Above us, the bug struggled, the lasso of magica straining and tearing, fighting to hold the monster against the boundary of the gate.

The hateful tones and harmonies shifted in the throat of the gate, forming a shape. No, an image. A woman, ethereal in shades of rippling red. She looked away from me as if surveying a landscape: Portland, burning and ruined and diseased. Her hair flowed down to her waist and twirled around her as she turned and locked eyes with me, smiling cruelly.

"Adia, you've lost," she growled in my mind. "This one you trusted, and this one won't sing!"

She knew. She knew exactly who I was. How I failed.

Deliver the final note, Claire, Adia echoed. I wasn't sure if she was still with me, or if she was gone, leaving me with only memory.

Well, she didn't say it had to be a *good* note. I inhaled.

And I screamed.

The waves of chaos and discord shredded apart at the force of my voice. The braids of magica snapped, and the bug fell. For a single heartbeat, the woman gawked, then she dissipated as the monster's body fell into the gate.

The Exalted Harmony became white noise, like a radio tuned between stations, the unshaped sound of cosmic rays and raw magica. Above it, I heard Adia's laugh, serene and beatific, as she spoke.

Be reborn, my maidens!

At the exact point where the first molecule of the bug's thaumatite touched the first particle of chaos magic in the gate, a white sphere sparked into existence and grew, as slowly as snow rolling into a ball. I realized we were seeing this in a dreamy, magic-induced slow motion. I watched calmly, almost sleepily, as the sphere grew to encompass the entire gate, then the monster, and finally reached us.

It moved so slowly that I almost accepted the inevitability of it before I felt myself fly backward from the bow shock of the explosion.

Enormous, glittering shafts of magica beamed out from behind the sphere, stretching over the entire city. The shockwave rippled across the sky and tore apart the rain clouds. Downtown Portland was suddenly bathed in stunning, glorious sunlight, a light shining upon a changed world, a world that now knew magical girls were real.

At some point, I sensed I was plummeting to the ground, with no magica left to cushion my fall. It seemed like cruel irony to have survived the end of the world, only to be killed by something as mundane as gravity. My vision dimmed, and I counted a small blessing that I'd be unconscious before I impacted the pavement.

If it had to end this way, well, at least I'd done what I needed to do.

* * *

I woke up in the middle of the street, exhausted and very, very sore, but conspicuously alive.

Sirens and shouting filled the air. I raised my head and looked around, trying to get my bearings. To my left stood the familiar sight of Howell's Bookstore at Tenth and Burnside, which meant I landed five blocks north of the Grand Sovereign; to my right lay the massive, oozing carcass of a giant dead bug monster blocking the entire street.

And standing above me was Bloom.

"Claire," she said. "You're not dead."

I pushed myself up on my elbows. "Is that relief or disappointment in your voice?"

"I'm still trying to figure out these ... *feelings*, so don't go quizzing me just yet." She sighed and rolled her eyes. "I'm not sad you're alive." With a nod and a pout, she looked down at me. "How's that?"

"I'll take what I can get. I really didn't think I was going to make it."

"Your little pals got tossed in every direction, but you looked worse off than the rest. I figured they could take care of themselves, but as for you—"

"Thank you for saving me."

She waved dismissively. "Yeah, yeah. This does *not* mean we're friends. Understand?"

I laughed. "That's fair. I have to say, it's nice to see the real you, Bloom."

"What are you talking about?"

I smiled at her as I got back on my feet. "We all spent time in our various closets, and now that we're out, we don't want it to end until we've lived as much of our lives as possible. That's how you feel too, isn't it? I can tell you're at least a little relieved to be free of Rennia."

"Pretty words, but they're easy for you. This isn't even my body. What—" She stopped and shook her head, her lip trembling.

I sighed. "It makes you feel like you're just an occupant, watching somebody else's existence happen to you."

"That is annoyingly accurate," she said, wiping her eye. "I learned a few things about you, thanks to Iris's connection to the Maidensong, so I know you're not just spouting empty platitudes."

"Definitely not. I felt like that until I became myself."

"Magical girls," she laughed. "Sappy and earnest to a fault. I'll say this for you, Claire: you are maddeningly nice."

"I'm going to choose to take that as a compliment."

A disc of magica materialized beneath her feet as she prepared to fly off, but she hesitated. "I need to figure out what this all means while I've still got the use of a body. We'll see what comes after that. I think I'd like to find my own property, if you know what I mean."

"Sara will be happy to hear that you don't want to live there permanently."

She paused for a moment, as if listening to a faraway voice. "Do something for me, would you?"

"What's that?"

"Tell Sara that Iris says she's very proud of her. And of you."

"I'll do that," I smiled, "and thank you."

She tensed up for launch, but then, she looked back at me.

"Hey, Claire?"

"Yeah?"

"Why a scream?"

I chuckled and shook my head. "I just couldn't think of anything else to do."

For the first time, I saw her smile without malice.

A moment later, she shot off into the sky. I watched her as she disappeared over the buildings of downtown ...

... which is when I realized that crowds were gathering, and were now staring at and filming me. The lenses of dozens of smartphones trained on me all at once.

The old, familiar knot of anxiety twisted up in my stomach. Whatever else had happened today, I wasn't exactly prepared to act as Magica Riot's public relations rep.

Fortunately, I was saved by the timely arrival of friendly faces.

Hazel ran out from the crowd of onlookers and threw her arms around me, squeezing me with crushing force.

"I saw everything from down on the street. Claire, that was incredible!"

I hugged her back. After blowing up a portal to another dimension and getting blasted five blocks away, holding Hazel felt like a thousand joys. "So, I guess you don't mind dating a magical girl?"

She laughed and reached up to give me a soft, slow kiss. "Are you kidding? I'm very okay with dating a magical girl." She relaxed but kept her arm tight around me. "I'm just going to have to keep hold of you, so you don't disappear."

I nuzzled against her. "I'm not going to, I promise."

The crowd parted as the rest of the girls emerged, bloodied and beaten but still standing. Nova pushed her way out in front and shot me an enormous grin.

"Y'know, babe, one of these days you're gonna have to stop passin' out on the street! It can't be good for ya!"

"Wasn't my first choice," I said.

Sara looked up in the direction Bloom had flown off. "I see she didn't stay."

"I think we'll see her again soon, when she's ready to find her own body. She wanted you to know that Iris is proud of you."

She smiled softly, tears glinting in her eyes. "Thank you. When she comes back with Iris, we'll figure something out."

I looked around at the damage to the city and the bug carcass towering over the street. In the distance, the unfinished hulk of the Grand Sovereign Hotel was now conspicuously nine stories shorter than before.

"So, did we, uh ... win?"

Sara smiled. "We won. The gate was completely destroyed."

"Corruption energy's gone, too," Cass said.

"Yep," Hana nodded. "That explosion knocked out all the creatures that came through the portals! It's like it zapped their batteries."

"It had to have been a massive shock to anything using Pandora energy," Sara said.

"That's good," I said. "I don't think I have much fight left in me today."

"Ain't that the flammin' truth," Nova laughed. "Time to kick back a little!"

"Does this mean you're done swearing?" Hana asked.

Nova puffed up with pride. "Eh, I think my word's more fun!"

The crowds around us were getting closer, staring either at us or at the massive bug corpse that was slowly coating the intersection of Tenth and Burnside with thick black pan-dimensional goo.

"Guess the secret is really out," I said.

Hazel gave me a squeeze. "Magica Riot is going to be front-page news everywhere on the planet. I don't know how all this works, but you probably can't sweep something like this under the rug!"

Cass laughed. "Yeah, I think that ship sailed."

"Soooooo, what's that mean for us?" Nova asked.

Sara shrugged. "I think we're going to be making it up as we go."

"I think you're right," Hana grinned. "The Alliance is going to be *very* busy now."

Nova pointed toward the crowd. "Uh, I think we are, too!"

People were approaching us from all sides with looks of curiosity or confusion on their faces. Which seemed entirely fair, given what they'd just witnessed.

"Who are you?"

"Did you kill that thing?"

"You saved my life at the market!"

"Hey, aren't you that band?"

"What were those monsters?!"

We exchanged nervous glances; the band was used to attention, but being recognized for our magical girl activities was something entirely different.

"Looks like our lives are going to get even more complicated from now on," Sara said.

Hazel perked up and stepped out in front of us, beaming a huge grin. "Sounds to me like you girls need a manager!"

"A manager?" Cass asked.

"Well, we have a commander," Hana said.

"No, no, a manager!" Hazel said. "Somebody to help you deal with the public and book gigs and stuff! Somebody who knows Portland, the local scene, bars and clubs, all that. Somebody who can help you deal with all this newfound fame."

"That makes sense, Hazel babe," Nova said. "You know anybody?"

I laughed. "I think I know what she's saying."

Hazel smiled and nodded. "Take me to your commander. I've got an offer she can't refuse!"

EPILOGUE

Four Weeks Later

EPILOGUE

| 19 |

I looked at myself in the dressing room mirror for the fifth or sixth time and straightened the lavender bow I'd put in my hair. Being kind to myself and my appearance was still a new concept, but as I looked at my reflection, in the purple and pink floral dress I'd first worn to Hazel's photo shoot, I finally had to admit the facts: I looked cute, actually and honestly. Tears welled up in my eyes. I caught myself before I let them get out of hand, lest I ruin my makeup.

"Hey, babe! You okay over there?" Nova asked from her seat on the other side of the greenroom, where she'd just finished sticking her thigh highs in place with fabric tape.

I looked over at her and smiled. "Better than okay. How about you? Ready to do this?"

"You better flammin' believe it! I wanna get loud!" She got up and ran over, grabbing me for an intense hug.

Cass and Hana sat behind us on a well-worn leather couch, double-checking the tuning on their instruments before de-materializing them back to the aetheric plane.

"Saw the crowd coming in after they opened the doors," Cass said. "They want loud, for sure."

Hana grinned. "Happy to oblige! Let's just hope this show doesn't get interrupted by any evil-doers."

"It's been a while since we got to play a whole set," Sara said. She leaned against the wall near the door, sipping a beer with a look of quiet thoughtfulness on her face. "Actually, I guess the last time was the Clarion Room."

"The night of Claire's awakening," Hana said. "What a nice symmetry!"

"That wasn't actually *that* long ago," I pointed out.

Cass shook her head. "Somebody really laid the old 'may you live in interesting times' curse on us."

"Lucky us," Sara chuckled. "At least we gave Dr. Barrera and Saoirse a lot of data."

At the back of the room, Commander McCoy sat on the edge of a table, drinking from a glass of whiskey. "You gals handled those interesting times like real pros. Looks like things are a little more settled tonight. What're you seeing on the scans, Agent Tomori?"

In a beanbag chair in the corner beside the commander, Hikari—the mumbling, black-clad, cyan-haired IT contractor we'd met at Big Pink while fixing that sensor weeks before—stared into the glow of their beat-up laptop and nodded almost imperceptibly. "Scans-wise nothing's showing up so far chief no Pandora readings nothing else looks like it's all quiet on the Pacific Northwestern front right now."

I leaned back and spoke softly to Hana. "It was genius to give Hikari's sticker to the commander."

"Well, the commander did say she was lonely," Hana said, "and we needed a computer tech. And Hikari clearly wanted a new job. Now that the Alliance is staffing up Portland again, it was a perfect fit!"

Despite our discretion, Hikari seemed to have excellent hearing. "Yeah believe me hacking the planet for a squad of literal magical girls is more interesting than fixing copiers for people who think 'brand strategy' and 'synergy' and 'core competency' are things humans should say anyway I'm here now I'm living it I'm loving it."

"I knew you were a good kid," the commander said. "How about comms? Any calls or messages I need to know about?"

"Oh well you know those fly fast and loose pretty much all the time now chief there's so many reporters and politicians and stuff in here like the mayor and city council and the governor and senators and somebody from the president's office yeah you've got a few waiting on you also the cops but I sent those to the junk folder."

The commander grinned. "Good call."

"It's not surprising," Sara said. "The government has no idea what to do with the existence of magical girls and monsters."

"And that's just the stuff they *do* know about," Cass added.

Nova laughed nervously. "It's gonna be a pain dealing with all this stuff, huh?"

Hikari looked up from their laptop. "There's a booking request to have you come play at the new Kaiju Carcass Food Cart Pod I guess that's for your new manager also Sara there's another message in here for you from that Allison Webb lady that keeps messaging she seems very persistent."

Hana shook her head. "What's her deal? She's messaged all of us, multiple times."

"I think she's government, too," Sara said. "Or, I don't know, military? Intelligence?"

The commander nodded. "Somethin' like that. I get big three-letter-government-agency vibes off her."

I shrugged. "Maybe she's just a fan?"

"Not calling with code tango charlie, she's not," the commander said. "Not with Alpha clearance."

"Oh, yeah, right, code tango charlie, of course," I said, not knowing even in the slightest what that meant.

Sara nodded slowly, seemingly turning the problem around in her head. "Whatever she wants, let's keep our distance for now."

Hikari perked up from the bean bag chair. "Oh hey Claire before I forget," they said as they threw something at me; it bounced off my head and landed on the floor with a hollow skitter.

I picked it up. It was a small purple USB stick.

"That's got a bunch of modules for your keyboard," Hikari continued. "They won't help you at all in combat but like they'll deliver that tasty '90s lead sound you've been craving it's a real aesthetic such that will totally make all the girls in the crowd swoon in a rock sense."

I laughed. "Thanks. I bet Hazel will appreciate that."

The greenroom door clicked and swung open, revealing Hazel standing in the doorway, holding a tablet.

"You know I already get feelings when you play!" She beamed at us. "Alright! It's a packed house out there. Officially the fastest sell-out in Daedalus Theater history!"

"Dang," Cass said. "Nice going, new manager. We're gonna have to start booking bigger venues, aren't we?"

Hazel nodded. "I'm already working on that, too! Turns out being a magical girl band is a good way to draw a crowd. In the meantime, we're ready to roll tonight. Sound engineer's got everything dialed in. Hikari's already recording the board. We've got press photographers and camera crews on-site, too. You can head to the stage anytime!"

Sara smiled. "Guess we better not keep them waiting. Huddle up!"

The rest of us stood, and we formed a circle in the center of the room, arms around each other's shoulders.

"To say the last few months have been a typhoon would be an understatement," Sara said, "but we did it. We saved people, made the world a better place. This wasn't our first fight, and it surely won't be the last, but for now ... let's go give that crowd a show they won't forget."

With a quiet exchange of looks and nods, we broke, and followed Hazel out of the greenroom and down the long, creaky wood hallway leading to the stage. When we reached the stage door, Hazel stopped me and planted a kiss on my lips.

"I'm so proud of you," she said as she pulled away.

I felt myself blush. "Aw, thanks, Haze."

"Go knock 'em dead, rock star."

I took a deep breath as Sara swung the door open and led us out.

The room exploded with cheers and applause. Twelve hundred people crammed in together, wanting to watch the band who'd saved the world. The sheer volume caught me off-guard, and I stopped for a moment, taking in the raw energy of the audience.

I knew there would be many more challenges ahead, a universe of magic that would throw threats and dangers at us that I couldn't possibly imagine yet. But here and now, there was music, and there would always be music. The music we made, and the music of the Maidensong, would guide us into that unwritten future.

I moved to my spot on stage. Sara turned back to us and smiled, and in unison, the five of us called forth our instruments in bright flashes of magica. The entire crowd gasped in surprise.

"Hey, friends," Sara said into her microphone as she looked out across the room. "Thanks for coming. We're Magica Riot!"

MAGICA RIOT
WILL RETURN

About the Author

Kara Buchanan is a former city planning journalist turned fiction author. After a dozen years writing about urban issues for various publications in her hometown, she moved to the Pacific Northwest and found the opportunity to come out of the closet and be her real self. Taking her love of magical girl anime, her time playing in bands, and her personal experiences dealing with gender issues, she created Magica Riot to bring a joyful, action-packed story of LGBTQ self-discovery and adventure to the world.

She lives in a modest house with a pretty garden, with her wife and three cats.

MAGICA RIOT

KARA BUCHANAN

www.ingramcontent.com/pod-product-compliance
Ingram Content Group UK Ltd.
Pitfield, Milton Keynes, MK11 3LW, UK
UKHW020642020625
6183UKWH00029B/278